THE BEGINNING OF THE EAST

THE BEGINNING OF THE EAST

by

MAX YEH

FICTION
COLLECTIVE
TWO

BOULDER • NORMAL

Published by Fiction Collective Two with support given by the English
Department Publications Unit of Illinois State University, the English
Department Publications Center of the University of Colorado at
Boulder, the Illinois Arts Council, and the National Endowment for the
Arts

Address all inquiries to: Fiction Collective Two, % English Department
Publications Center, University of Colorado at Boulder, Boulder, CO
80309-0494

The Beginning of the East
Max Yeh

ISBN: Cloth, 0-932511-62-7
ISBN: Paper, 0-932511-63-5

Produced and printed in the United States of America
Distributed by the Talman Company

Book Design: Jean C. Lee
Cover/Jacket Design: Dave LaFleur

DEDICATION

He was perched on his motorcycle in the photograph, facing back-wards, his left leg curled under him on the BMW's fat seat, his other leg hanging down touching the ground, balanced, on his head the Guatemalan skullcap he always wore in the mornings, its purple, orange, red, yellow, white stripes turned into grey and black blurred densities in the blowup we had made of his head. His expression is all wrong, his look is askance, sad, the scar on his cheek showing but nothing of the smile or the life, but there he is, still, beautiful, beautiful, he always said, these people are beautiful, and I'm so lucky, so lucky that they let me come here just to see it all, it gets better the farther south you go, all the way down, you just go, that's all, no hay problemas. He had been through Guatemala, yes, you just hold up your hands and say, no hay problemas, and in El Salvador had hung out with an American film crew, there they were in the middle of the war on the beach filming who knows what, but was finally turned back at the canal under the hot, humid heat, sweating in the black helmet they made him wear, though here in Mexico he could go without and would, taking windy rides through the Chiapas mountains, winding and winding back and forth as he had done in the Alps when his company gave him a month's vacation to decide which vice-presi-dency in the ad company he wanted to take over, and he decided to do what he had always wanted to do and that was to ride his bike in the Alps; so he shipped his BMW to Switzerland and began crossing the Alps, the yellow and red flower-covered mountains, the high passes and sunny vistas, crossing not once but twenty times from west to east and back, from north to south and back, and pretty soon he had put 10,000 miles on the bike, the gears still clunking in that characteristic BMW way; so he shipped his bike to Mexico, wrote his friend John that he was quitting the company, started procedures to sell the house he and his wife still owned together, a small, very fine-boned woman, we're still friends, and very beautiful, but the daughter, she's terrific, beautiful, she's got green hair and writes rock and roll and has a punk rock band, she's a groupie, all I love is rock and roll, yeah, just be calm, life is too precious to lose by getting upset, see? you just go and no hay problemas. All the young people reminded him of his daughter, like Magdalena, whose sister was also named Magdalena, in fact her two sisters both, she's a bit shy, you know, scared inside, but she's all right, just give her a little encouragement, and like Antonio, with whom he sat for hours talking excitedly, both of them laughing, gesticulating, telling stories, vroom, vroom, phttt, y no hay problemas, which seemed to us so odd, since he only knew four or five phrases in Spanish and Antonio refused ever to speak or listen to English, which he thought an ugly language, but hour after hour with Antonio, who was very together, very fine, and so young, he talked, his heart sometimes crumbling because here in the dry, fragrant mountains with frost every morning he found he was no longer a left over of the 60s. His plank bed, the magic sleeping bag that never let him get cold, an oil-can stove that every night brought visitors into his resin-scented hut with drums and guitars and once a flute and a violin, and always a bottle of Pastis, Hecho en Mexico but como el verdadero pastis de Marsella, were all he needed besides, of course, his darling BMW that took him on his trips to Agua Azul and the land of magic mushrooms growing above the falls in a cow pasture, the lush jungle vegetation steaming and the mist from the falls glistening in a multi-colored haze above, against the deep blue sky when he lay on his back, listening, listening to the rock and roll in his head, as he lay on the hot pavement in Guatemala, just over the border in late spring, his last trip before going back north to Canada, listening and listening until he died.

To Bill, then, this rite de passage is dedicated, in memoriam but also in exchange for the Hostess Munchies yellow monster watch, a vestige of his former life as an advertising executive, which Bill gave my daughter, which didn't work until last year, when Rihan was finally old enough to tell time and one afternoon I leaned over it taking the watch to pieces, sorting out the gears, lined up all the pieces, meshed them, held them all in their appointed and linked places over and over again while I tried to fit them all into the case again and again, all engaged and in their order, spaced, so concentrated that when I looked up from the ticking watch it was dark, my neck and back ached, my eyes felt folded in on themselves and every time I moved my head a pain stretched down from my skull. Now Rihan tells time with it, though it is a little fast.

PART ONE
MEXICO CITY

...unde spericus sperica spericum idest rotundus
& solidus ad modum spere.

—*Columbus*

1

ome buildings leaned over and slowly sank like great ships, their windows flashing the clear, bright sky, tracing huge arcs with their rays of reflected sunlight across the faces of the surrounding buildings: others, touched by some powerfully magic wand, simply disintegrated in mid-air, their firmness all gone, became for a moment hovering forms of dust, shivering mirages of their former beings, and then collapsed into piles of rubble. Whole floors were sliced away, while those above and below remained intact, so that the buildings looked stunted brothers of themselves, the only sign of their past the loops of bent girders sticking out the corners where once there had been a fifth or sixth floor. Top floors became small garbage dumps, dull, colorless masses of broken glass, bent aluminum frames, bricks, rocks, tangles of iron rods, contrasting with the elegant glass and concrete structures that held them high in the air. Brightly painted walls, blue, brown, maroon, green, ochre, yellow, black, red, orange, turquoise, olive, grey, crackled, flaked, peeled, dulled, and aged, pieces of their masonry jutting out or fallen or falling. High up on these expansive and dilapidated cliffs, he saw bathrooms appear suddenly, shining yellow tile work, gold-trimmed shower stall, a bottle of shampoo still balanced on the stall's edge, a coatrack in the corner behind the toilet with its seat left up by the master of the house, a brown bathrobe blowing slightly in the warm breeze as if it were really real and not the dollhouse miniature it seemed, or he saw until the heavy gas from the tanks on top the buildings slowly leaking down ventilators and stairwells and drainpipes found the hot water heaters in the apartments below and with a sudden blue flash of lightning followed by clouds of dust the buildings disappeared with their peaceful and comfortable doll-house furniture, miniature bookshelves with even tinier books that actually opened, tinware pans, enameled stove, handknit rugs, small portraits and landscapes painted with human hair brushes hanging on the papered walls.

That morning their apartment had given the illusion of slowly tipping over to an incomprehensible angle and then suddenly and silently began snapping back and forth with such violence that he could not get his key into the shifting doorlock to get out, poking and jamming the key about while he hung onto the knob, Carol saying, open the door, open the door, and then, pick her up, pick her up, for Christ's sake, when he realized that he was dragging his daughter down the stairs bouncing like a ragged doll, and then the earthquake was over, up the street a bit of dust rising where they had been doing some construction for two weeks, some few people standing on the street with the three of them, their neighbor from below on the fourth floor driving up and asking if they had seen his wife. The sun shone, the sky was blue, so he hurried Carol and Rihan upstairs, chuckling about Rihan's bruised shins, their fright or lack of it, how quiet it was, how quickly and yet how slowly it developed, how they had to hurry to get to school on time, where each one was when the realization came, he in the bathroom, Carol in the kitchen, Rihan trying to eat her breakfast, as she had to do now quickly, remembering the quakes in California, the time at night when they woke up to see all the bric-a-brac off the shelves crashing about, how bizarre and unthreatening the shaking seemed to Rihan who expected the earth to swallow the apartment building as the earthquake did Dorothy and Zeb.

Even at Rihan's school, with the discussions about the crack on the building across the street and half the teachers absent and the children saying where were you, he had not known that something really extraordinary had happened and planned to go home as soon as he could get Rihan into class, to arrange to meet Beto that afternoon in Santa Anita. He had found in the quiet, empty reading room of the French Library a study of Latin American urban slums which included a map of Mexico City, and although it did not discuss Santa Anita, the map gave some interesting information about the types of construction there ten years ago. But at home the radio was full of excited chatter, a man seen running naked down the street, motorcycles sent out in brigades, telephone calls coming in saying everything is fine here, so that at last Carol said she was going out to find out what was happening, but he stayed in, reminded of the curious radio reports he listened to after Kennedy's assassination about a giant rabbit or was it a clown or a man dressed as a rabbit named Oswald appearing here and there in Dallas, then in other parts of Texas, and, he remembered, in Mexico, until finally he, too, went into the streets with the thousands of people walking up and down the Reforma, some crowded in front of leaning buildings, others, whole families, walking very fast as if going somewhere though there was nowhere to go, muttering or shouting aimlessly out loud, millions, millions of dollars, what destruction, and one man in striped pajamas and leather slippers covered with dust trying unsuccessfully to flag down a cab.

That evening he sat in front of his apartment window watching the city burn, every few minutes the skyline lit up with a slow, rosy explosion, another propane tank, while the radio, transformed from its usual mercantile tonalities, was alive with people's real voices, describing their escapes with wonder and excitement, asking for help with urgency and faith, giving advice humbly, voices giving encouragement, voices offering information, voices talking, voices responding, crying voices, cheering voices, mostly young voices, confident and efficient. In the street behind his building he saw a stream of commandeered buses, taxis, old VWs, beaten and scarred Chevrolets and Fords, going to and from the rescue center that had been set up in the abandoned railroad workers' hospital in the next block. There were no official vehicles and none of the fancy cars that he usually saw during a normal rush hour.

Carol went out the next day to work with the volunteers. He stayed home with Rihan, whose school would be closed for the next two months. He could not phone Beto, but he had been to two of the photo processors he used, both places were gone, rubble, nothing left, big piles of broken bricks and mortar, Doña Rosa would be busy with the problems in Santa Anita because even if the quake hadn't brought down any buildings on them, the slums would have no water or electricity, Beto's father's building was probably down, according to the radio reports it was in the center of the damage, and they would have to move out right away, so the article on slum architecture in Santa Anita had to be set aside for a while, which was fine because he couldn't leave Rihan alone anyway.

But it was not fine, because the libraries were closed and thirty years of scholarship, research, and teaching had fixed in him an insatiable habit of reading, not just pleasurable and imaginative reading but a kind of prying, searching reading, at once quick and analytic. He read the way he watched television, hypnotically, in large doses, not caring what programs he watched but always with fixed attention and detailed recall, so when the newspapers returned to the stands, he bought as many as he could, not just the Mexico City papers but journals and magazines from other Latin American countries and even some trade journals. He spent the days cooking and reading the papers, ten to twelve hours a day, though even then he could not keep up and the papers collected around the apartment in piles unread.

He read, in his usual way, all the articles and most the want ads, jotting down notes, especially delighting in unexpected connections. Once he read a letter to the editor in *Uno Mas Uno* deploring an unfair critique of a new American book on the contemporary Mexican novela, the letter writer mentioning that *Uno Mas Uno*'s reporter had accused the American professor of arrogant behavior at the public panel discussion of his book, whereas the American had only said two things the whole evening, once to invite late-comers to take a seat and later to ask that there be no smoking. The letter writer went on to describe the reporter's behavior at the panel discussion, recounting that he had arrived late with another writer, had made obnoxious and jeering remarks in a stage whisper about the gringo and that the reporter's friend had finally leapt up interrupting the proceedings by declaring that he objected to the American professor's book because he was not included in it, even though he had written several novels and it was not his fault that they did not become famous and some of them were not even published. Then the reporter from *Uno Mas Uno* stood up and read a prepared statement listing all the writers whom the American professor had ignored. The two were finally pacified when one of the eminent panel members got up and extemporaneously listed more ignored writers.

He was still mulling over the implications of this letter, the points of view of all those involved, when he came upon an article by the eminent panel member of that literary evening, who it seems was inspired by the fracas to reminisce on the history of intellectual battles, describing the many times enraged intellectuals had punched out their opponents, as he had recently done at the home of a famous novelist, knocking down not one but two of his nemeses and kicking them for good measure. And, indeed, on the very next page of the newspaper, he found an article by that voluble, ignored novelist friend of the *Uno Mas Uno* reporter, who had caused such a ruckus at the panel discussion, describing his encounter for the first time with a famous writer and their encouraging discussion of his forthcoming novel. Yes, he had been taken to the famous novelist's home by that eminent panel member who had there punched out his enemies, though this last event was left out of the article. Below this article, he found another, which completed satisfactorily his search. The *Uno Mas Uno,* reporter and critic, friend of the ignored novelist, reviewed, rather negatively, the first two issues of a new literary journal, edited by the two unfortunate invitees to the famous writer's dinner party.

Such closures pleased him by their heroic stand against the purely accidental and meaningless nature of events. They made history out of journalistic incidents, yet they had the comedic quality of the purely fortuitous coincidence, like the casting of the yarrow-stalks, or like the fine arc of Jeannette Clochard's fall through space when she jumped from the south tower of the Notre Dame cathedral in Paris and, instead of killing herself as she intended, landed on June McAllister, an American tourist, killing her. This was in 1962, he remembered. It would be nice if Professor McAllister, whose book on Mexican novelas he had skimmed the last time he was at the American Library just before the quake, had had a sister named June.

But the problem with information, he quickly found, was that there was too much of it, that availability created its own problems, problems he never faced while living in the US, for there, for numerous reasons, some financial, others decorous, news information, especially about international politics, was largely government controlled. How this came about was, perhaps, instructive. During the financial crisis of the 1970s, American news bureaus all over the world were discontinued, only a few large agencies continuing to provide foreign news, so that during the Carter years neither the *New York Times* nor the *Washington Post* had reporters in Central America, all information about the El Salvador war during a period of major debate about American funding in Central America being provided by the American Embassy in San Salvador. But economics were not the real reason the foreign news services were closed, because they were not in fact more costly than local news services, only, the information services decided, less of interest to the American public. Further, large portions, sometimes as much as 80% of newspaper space in American papers was taken up by articles written for special interest groups and circulated by public relations firms. So the free press of the US results in much less information, much more orthodox points of view, is more susceptible to governmental control, and is more boring than this mass of information from all the conceivable news services of the world, including the Xinhua News Agency out of China, that he received here in this party-controlled and state-controlled society of Mexico.

By the second week of reading he had to confine himself to one paper a week, the telephones were working again, Beto had called twice, but he had put him off. It took two days to read through a paper thoroughly, but then he had to collate the information, he had collected so many clippings, so that in the rainy days of October, he laid the clippings out on the floor of the bedroom, converting it into an extended scrabble board. The day the electricity came on, so not only was the water problem somewhat solved but he could extend his reading hours into the evening, he found one of the pieces he was looking for. An analyst for Lloyd's Bank discovered that England had been pumping 80% more oil out of its North Sea fields than it needed and that the wells would last only 10 more years. He placed this article under the bed, in line with the articles, xeroxed at the French Library from their file of old newspapers, about the sudden drop in oil prices on the spot market, with the figures he had found from four-month-old papers showing the recent 40% drop in the American stockpile of oil, with the articles on the lowering of prices by OPEC and on Mexican losses of revenue that resulted from the drop in prices, with the dates of the Iraqi bombing of Iranian oil works, and next to the news of the recent military coup in Nigeria which likely resulted in a government unwilling to maintain its oil production quota and thus likely to begin a price war.

The extension of this line surprised him. It argued a large, international conspiracy involving many governments, many agencies of many governments, many corporations, all acting in unison, fairly quickly and efficiently. He did not believe in conspiracy theories of history, his only interest at the moment being more aesthetic than anything else, just a fascination with the possible configurations of information, yet if he had to think conspiracy, though not all the information, not even a small part of the information, surely, was available to him, he would surmise that England and the US were engaging in a complicated and, for England, spectacular gamble to force the oil producers into economic bankruptcy and dependency, thus guaranteeing extended cheap prices for oil in the future, the principle being simply to flood the market at the present time, drive the prices down, buy oil back and stockpile the non-perishable oil while the prices are low, flood the market again and buy back again, each cycle being accompanied by complicated loan structures. During periods of high prices, the oil countries would be encouraged into modes of economic development and thus into taking large loans on future production, and when the prices dropped, the English and American banks could pressure the indebted nations to extend their loan periods, while the English and American oil companies stockpiled cheap oil. Eventually, all the oil will be indebted, when prices will have to remain low, because any rise in oil prices would increase world inflation and thus increase the interest rates on all loans, an impossible situation for any indebted nation, and except for the initial outlay, which England and the US have already committed, the cycles of selling and buying can be managed without a debit. From his information, the time plan for this process already seemed plain. England had only 18 years of petroleum left in the North Sea. By shortening that some three or four years, it guaranteed a much longer period of cheap oil on the world market. For the US, he imagined other motives besides cheap oil, since the gambit allowed the US to strike sidewise at Iran and at the same time to put short-term pressure on Venezuela and on Mexico to loosen their determination to organize the Latin American countries through the Contadora agreements.

Though he did not believe such a conspiracy was possible, he saw that an impartial collation of information dictated that he cross his line of clippings on oil with two other lines touching at Contadora and Central American news and again at Third World indebtedness. He had added a third dimension to his scrabble board, and now, having moved out of the bedroom, he was trying to use the furniture in some way to add another dimension, but he knew that that wasn't enough. He needed many dimensions, all able to touch. Touching was the issue, contiguity, continens the Latins called it with their superior-than-all, centrist minds, borrowing that from the Greeks, the world was all continens, in three touching, next to each other parts, whole and one and only, but of three continents. He tried to explain that to Rihan. The big pieces of land surrounded by water, those are continents, though not exactly, because originally it meant just the opposite. It all turned up-side-down with Columbus. You see these piles of clippings, they're the continents, and I'm just trying to get them to touch each other again: which was true since even though most the articles he read were political, his understanding of them was purely cartographic. He had never been much interested in what governments did to other governments or corporations to other corporations or armies to other armies, and during the Vietnam era, he had confined his activism to giving lectures on the relations between technical developments in targeting and modern carto-graphic methods. His piles of clippings were the visible signs of a method, abstract and meaningless in itself, which produced a system of relationships whose reality it guaranteed. It was better than viewing the world through green glasses, because the world it made, being tactile and tangible relations, was less visual and thus less illusory.

The earthquake had profoundly shaken people's inner being, so that when the after-shock struck the city in dark evening, they had fled through the streets screaming and sobbing. Even calm Rihan was touched by the woman crumpled in the middle of the street crying hysterically and had difficulty sleeping the weeks after, and once Carol telephoned to ask him to get her because she felt the ground so unstable she could not walk home. They and the elderly couple downstairs, who had told them they had been foolish to run out onto the street, were the only ones to stay in the apartment building. He had abandoned the Santa Anita project, just shopping, cooking, reading his newspapers and managing the apartment building.

In his attempt to save water, the toilet became his major enemy. When the electricity was off and he had to carry two buckets of water up five flights of stairs to use the toilet once, even after he had reduced the capacity by hanging a two liter plastic bag of water inside the reservoir, up five flights of stairs to get rid of a cup of odiferous, yellow liquid, he knew there was an insanity in it, but the toilet was insatiable. When the electricity returned, he caught the water from the shower in a tub, washing his hair first in the cold water that was in the pipes before the hot water came, turning off the water when he soaped, forcing everyone to shower together so the water in the pipes would not cool down, but even then the water from three of them showering was hardly enough for three flushes. When he collected the water from washing clothes, too, there was just enough water for the day, if they calculated their pissing rhythms correctly and didn't flush at all at night, the diapery greeting hitting them in the morning. The radio was begging people not to shower too often and to wear clothes longer between washes, but he was showering every day and washing his clothes every day just to keep the toilet happy.

Sitting on the toilet, waiting, looking at the plastic tub half full of grey water, he thought of his plumbing system at home in the US: he would have to redesign the system, run the drain pipes from the bathtub and the washer into a holding tank in the basement or into a separate septic and then hook up the pump that was in the barn, probably without its pressure tank, and hook it up to the toilet inlet line, he'd have to have a T and two gate valves there, so when there wasn't enough water in the holding tank he could switch to clean water, but in the final analysis the toilet really should go, this great sanitary invention that saved hundreds of thousands of Americans and Europeans from unknown but imaginable terrors, this symbol of the American, the Western way of life, cleanliness, sanitation, no pissing or shitting in the streets and behind bushes and fences as he had done as a child in China, learning early to squat in such a way that he kept himself clean, this product of a waterlogged nation of perpetual fogs and drizzles that he remembered approaching years ago on a French bus, approaching the channel and watching the great cloud bank slowly draw near.

The toilet will be the destruction of Mexico and of all other water-short, Third World countries, Mexico which every dry season already suffered major shortages and now with the earthquake having broken pipes in more than 4,000 places, needing, they said, three times the nation's total yearly earnings to replace and repair the system, so they can have their usual shortages again, will go broke, sell itself to American and European and maybe Japanese banks just to satisfy the toilets.

He had been taught, as most people in Europe and America, that technological inventions, like toilets, were commodious, which was nothing more than redundancy, since they were all based on what in high school he learned was called mechanical advantage, a little effort got you a lot of work done, so that the more of these inventions you used the less effort you had to expend yourself, and that was what most people thought was meant by the conservation of energy, but he could see that the work he did in carrying two buckets of water up the stairs, which was the work the electric pump usually saved him from doing, was work created by the toilet. If he didn't have the toilet but only an outhouse downstairs, that work would not be necessary, which meant that the work inventions saved was work the inventions created, and those ads he remembered nostalgically from his childhood in China of spotless kitchens, white enameled gas stoves, yellow-haired ladies in print dresses and cute little aprons, breathed a leisure that was deceptive.

But it was a shame about toilets, because he liked toilets: great jowls of toilets, prim receptacles of toilets, delicate little bowls, the porcelain forms were wonderfully various and organic, he had found once on a study tour of Germany, England, France, Switzerland, and Spain, so that at all the archives and libraries and institutes in Europe he had photographed the toilet bowls, specially designed ones to fit into corners, old fashioned, stately, and ornate ones, short, fat, squat ones, children-sized ones, tall, lean ones, and never two the same, some emphasizing their curving, sweeping, bowl-like innards by being molded into beautiful designs, swan's necks or griffin bodies, others hiding their mechanisms within non-committal geometries. He favored the old French, stand-up kind, though the German idea of a shelf to catch the stool to lessen the splash was good, too. The French model was more hygienic for public use, with their cross-hatched footprints that he matched his feet to, completing, as it were, a mirror image of the toilet, egress and ingress, so that squatting there he fulfilled a spatial expectancy, and when the water schlussed down from apparently nowhere, if the flow were adjusted properly, he marvelled at how the water swirled around the little islands that supported him and kept him dry, standing on water. But the alternatives to flush toilets, even setting aside the losses to his imagination, were difficult to contemplate, and though he had used an outhouse or a potty or a hedge until he was seven and remembered no aversion to it, forty years of American living had changed his olfactory sense, leaving him unable to appreciate the variations and harmonies of the wooden outhouse, a Japanese topos, and not believing the Swedish version, an odor-free, dry toilet, and suspecting the self-contained, fully recycling water and sewage unit to be merely technology inventing another toilet, requiring more labor and money to demonstrate its labor and money saving ways, in the end, creating work rather than lessening it, he had no alternative to offer: shit was shit, except the crisp vision of a Cathare toilet he had seen in Southern France, carved in stone, jutting out the side of a twelfth-century Albigensien stronghold, perched impossibly high on a pinnacle, so that the droppings fell some three hundred meters wind-blown down a sheer cliff face, through the deep blue sky of the meridian sun, probably already dried and odorless when they smashed into powder on the rocks below.

2

Like the cracked and crumbled buildings that revealed their secrets, falsified building permits, violated codes, children and women working like slaves in eighteenth-century conditions in dozens of sweatshops sewing Pierre Cardins, Bonjours, Gitanos, Calvin Kleins for the American market, police torturers crushed at detention centers along with their victims under a collapsing roof, while a portable television screen still projected news images of the devastated center of the city, outside the station in a car flattened by the wall it was parked behind, the body of a policeman and a journalist missing since three months ago, he too seemed to have opened up, suffering repeated internal aftershocks, like everyone else, or, perhaps, he did not so much open up as the world around him lost its accustomed solidity. He did not feel that he could smell and hear and see its coherence but only register its details, like some brain-damaged patients he had read about. Eastern and Western eschatology coincided, he thought, in associating the end of things with revelations. Out his apartment window, the city seemed in the daytime the same city as before the earthquake, but looking closely at them from his striped lawnchair, those familiar grey, pink, tan buildings, their familiar watertanks, the clotheslines, the zigzagging brickworks, he felt certain had somehow to be recreated. He felt an airiness, an overwhelming vastness of space, that isolated all the objects he saw. As a corollary, perhaps, he lost interest in his scholarly work, at least in the substance of his research, but he transfered all his habits of thinking, the inventions of research tools, the serendipitous methodology, the questing for sources, the speculations on origins to his new task of reconstruction.

He continued to sit in his lawnchair in front of the window, catching the smog-filtered sun, and read, anything and everything, voraciously, certain that his reading would eventually bring reality together again and glad that he was unburdened by the boredom that he knew drove other readers from the details that were essential to his method of work, so everything from statistics to political pamphlets to inconsequential anecdotes entered his compilations as starlike interstices of significance. That morning he read a declaration that had been given the Red Cross at the penal center of Mariona in El Salvador by someone who was a prisoner there, arrested on August 14, 1984, at the school (Republica Federal de Alemania) in San Salvador at 8:30, meeting with 22 other teachers to discuss matters having to do with ANDES 21 DE JUNIO, our teachers' association. I should mention that our association was juridical: that is, it was legally constituted, he noted. However, since in our country the right of public meeting is not respected, we were taken into custody like criminals or rebels. Our arrest and detention took place as a result of false accusations and assumptions on the part of the El Salvadoran Army. It was a commonplace account, like many he had read before, the streets were filled with political propaganda sheets like it, but now his net of interrelated events reached out to give these stories a home, as if they filled the empty spaces between relations with images of lives lived, verifying the abstract relations just as those relations gave the stories credibility, actually, he thought, more than that, because if the stories did not exist, the details of the relations he established would write the stories themselves. He had by now given up on his piles of clippings, and instead, kept a cross-referenced card file of the various topics of each article, cross-referenced according to names, places, dates, and sources, but most helpful of all were the diagrams he kept in a large, loose-leaf drawing pad, maps showing various relations of topics, also cross-referenced, but this time by color, so that the pad could be flipped through rather quickly and, like old-fashioned flickers, the dancing colors give an indication of the complex weaving of historical events.

From the moment I was arrested until I was sent to this detention center on the 27th of October, I was savagely tortured: that is, I was kept 75 days in a cell of the Policia de Hacienda, one of the many bodies within the Army which has charge of the arrest and assassination of people in this country who belong to social or political organizations or associations. Among the tortures used on me I can list these: being beaten with fists all over my body but primarily in the head and the stomach, being kicked all over, beatings with the barrel and the butt of a rifle in the body. He had been with some ten boys who beat a man in the dark city park one Halloween night, the dull thuds against the man's ribs deadened even more by the surrounding bushes, but he had never been beaten himself, so could not tell if he were scared of it, yet his temples ached from gritting his teeth when he thought of being hit in the head with a baseball bat. The hood was put on me, a kind of asphyxiation where my arms and legs were tied, the arms behind me. I was put face down with two police torturers sitting on my back, and the hood, a plastic bag, put over my face and head, depriving me of air. They brought me to when they saw I was dying, and when I caught my breath, he caught his breath, they repeated the torture. I was also kept hanging for whole nights from the ceiling of the cell I was kept in. My arms were tied behind my back, and I was hung up, so that my feet could not touch the floor. In addition to these things all the interrogations were carried on with verbal insults and outrages, vulgar and humiliating. During the 75 days he was kept by the Policia de Hacienda, I was tortured from about 2 hours to sometimes 18 hours a day, the interrogations were directed by an official from the Intelligence Department of the Chief of Staff of the Army. I could never identify him since I was always kept blindfolded in his presence. Nor could he identify his interrogators, or rather my torturers, since they always came with their caps pulled over their faces. Generally, the chief of the Policia de Hacienda, Colonel Franciso Moran, participated in the interrogations and tortures along with an Army officer. In one interrogation and torture, an American advisor participated. Since I was blindfolded I did not see him, but I concluded he was American by his foreign accent and by the fact that from time to time he spoke in English to the other torturers. Also, an adviser from Taiwan participated in several interrogations and tortures. Strange, what is a Chinese doing here, this time he saw him, but his face was covered by his cap, the official directing the interrogation told me that one of his companions, and he pointed to him, was from Taiwan. The presence of the American adviser correlated with reports he had from 1968, he had started extending his readings into newspaper archives, when the Mexican police raided the headquarters of the Young Communists, a completely legal political organization in Mexico, all the prisoners being first interrogated by an American Embassy staff member to discover the names and addresses of Mexican Americans who had friends or relatives in the Mexican Communist Party, even before they were questioned by the Mexican authorities, and correlated also with a bizarre instance of American presence, a reminder of what America represented in the minds of Mexicans, also from the student disturbances of 1968, when a student being beaten by the police during an interrogation and asking why he was being beaten for having been only a bystander was told that if the Mexicans didn't beat him the gringos would be down doing it. The presence of the Chinese puzzled him until he found the news item reporting a statement from the Reagan White House during one of the Congressional debates on American aid to El Salvador claiming that the debate was merely academic since the government had already received two offers from Asian countries to channel covert funding.

He continued to read that the daily tortures took place at regular times, usually at night. And what made it worse was that the torturers almost always got high on marijuana or liquor or both before they began, which I knew was happening because I could smell the marijuana smoke and the alcohol. Also, sometimes when they took my blindfold off I saw the bottles of liquor. I always said to my torturers that it was unjust that they should torture and humiliate me in that way when my only crime seemed to be that I was an officer of the teachers' association of El Salvador. I always told myself I had to get out from all this abuse and outrage to which I was submitted, but I despaired when I saw that the handcuffs that manacled my hands, the rifles with which they beat me, the spotlights they shone in my eyes, and on and on, were all made in the United States, and all the time I asked myself why a great people does nothing to keep its government from complicity in such savage and abominable doings.

He turned to the end of the declaration, wondering about the signature, Walter Zuleta Osorio: who was Walter Zuleta, and why did this poor, victimized school teacher carry the name of a Teutonic knight, ruler of hosts, did his family for generations pass down the name of some pirate raider, follower of Francis Drake or Walter Ralegh, or was his name just another example of American hegemony, and if it were so, what an irony, and if it were not, he could be sure that the name would still be some aftermath of a dimple in international history. Would he recognize Walter Zuleta if he ever met him, did it matter whether the person whose story, life, he was considering was named Walter or Christopher or Max, was he telling the truth, was there such a person, did that matter? He read, besides the physical tortures I received, I also suffered psychological and moral tortures. During the 75 days I was completely isolated from the outside world. He was in a cell without ventilation or illumination, two small holes in which were night and day and the rest empty darkness, the door sealed. I forgot to say that on three occasions I was drugged: I was made to inhale the fumes from rags soaked in paint thinner. In the cell in which I was kept, I had access to nothing, nothing to read, no one to talk to, the door being opened only to give me food. And this was another punishment, since several times I was left for as long as three days without food, and when they heard his desperate cries asking for food, they gave me a hard tortilla with sour beans: that was all, and that was the way it always went.

The cell was plagued with insects, fleas, lice, millipedes, cockroaches, scorpions, flies, mosquitoes, beetles, centipedes, spiders, and others. There was a permanent stink that made me vomit. The mattress I slept on smelled pestilential and had a fungal growth that infected my body. During the 75 days, I stayed in the same clothes which I had on the day I was arrested. I was not allowed to bath the first 30 days. Many times when I asked to urinate or to defecate, they did not take me to the facilities, and I had to hold myself in, since they threatened to beat me if I did what I had to do where I was.

An event which brought me anguish and horror was that on Monday the 16th of August, they arrested one of my sisters and her husband. I discovered this on Wednesday the 18th when they brought my sister to my interrogation. I did not see her since I was blindfolded, but we talked. She insinuated that she had been beaten and threatened with death. The crime which they were accused of was that I lived in their house, which was certainly true. I was morally destroyed when I found out that they had been arrested. I cried to see that for something so insignificant, that is for the fact of belonging to an organization of my own country, I had suffered the near torture of seeing my family tortured. Only in this country do governments commit uncivilized acts. How is it possible that my family suffers for the fact that I belong to a legal and recognized organization? Now while I am here in this jail, I hear that during this whole period the houses of my seven brothers have been under continual surveillance by the Policia de Hacienda. My family in general has been threatened with the loss of work because of pressures from the Army.

It did not seem to matter if Zuleta's testimony was true or not. The correlations between his story and the patterns of Central American politics in no way proved his story, but they gave his experiences a cast of reality, so that it became evident to him that truth and accuracy may not have anything to do with reality. He had seen this in ancient maps, which not having the accuracy produced by crisscrossing, bouncing lasar beams used today, nevertheless conjured up real worlds of travel, adventure, danger, and home. Perhaps it was another example, like toilets, of the futility of technology, accuracy in mapmaking only generating its own need for more accuracy without creating a greater reality, he would have to remember that. In any case, the relation's reality was more certain to him than the buildings on the other side of his window. It didn't matter if Zuleta lied or if he did not even exist, the story being made up for propaganda reasons, though this assumption bothered him when he considered that Zuleta might have truly suffered, because whoever wrote this piece imagined pain and humiliation as uneventful, ordinary, quotidian existence, unjust, but there to live through as part of an everyday reality, and simple, that touched him, the simplicity of the story, because in the US we dramatize torture, not so much because we are free of violence but because, he thought, we prefer to think ourselves free of it, so that the images, fabricated or real, that we conjure up are so outrageous, so extravagant that they seem to relieve us of our responsibility for them. Zuleta's captors did not connect electrodes to his gonads, as Argentineans are reported to have done, nor did they force a rat into his anus, as the Colombian mafia are said to do, but his tortures, plain and daily repeated, were more terrifying being less dramatic, so that even if it were all fictional, the indignation was certain, as it was certain that the indignation was directed at whatever happens every day in El Salvador.

He had forgotten, perhaps he never knew, what everyday life was like for non-Americans and non-Europeans, for the vast majority of the people of the earth, for Chinese, too, he supposed, and that meant for him, too, whose lives were always subject in the smallest details to the incomprehensible forces not only of nature and gods but of American or European actions, so that the cartoonish map of San Salvador he had seen in the window of the Texas International Air agency, showing in exaggerated three-dimensional fore-shortening all the buildings of American corporations, MacDonald's, IBM, Xerox, Kodak, Chrysler, General Motors, Bank of America, Coca Cola, American Express, Mastercard, Visa, Ford, Caterpillar, John Deere, Cummins, T.I.A., Kimberly Clark, Dole, Winthrop, Lilly, Colgate-Palmolive, General Tire, looming over the city, may have some truth to it. He had certainly not remembered when he ducked out of the rainstorm this past summer under the green and yellow awning outside Sullivan's Bar and Grill and had been buttonholed by a paunchy, slightly drunk American explaining the need in Mexico for the latest counter-insurgency techniques he was here to sell, having retired as a green beret training officer, techniques, such as keeping prisoners in suspended cages, which had been tested in Vietnam and would constitute the backbone of Mexican national defense in the southern states when and if Central America fell, had forgotten or did not know, that this obnoxious but curious example of free enterprise, this internationalized update of Willy Loman, would end up, one day, part of someone's, some non-American's, everyday life, perhaps, end up in Walter Zuleta's narration, a consideration which confirmed, once again, the substantiating power of his mapping of current events. He was making the schemas for everyday reality, giving form, direction and distance, to the rivulets, forests, and hills of life.

The men who arrested me, beat and humiliated me, he continued, used a series of publicity tricks to justify my detention to the public. They gathered evidence that I owned propaganda of all kinds from revolutionary organizations in this country, which was and is totally false. They said I belonged to the Salvadoran guerrilla movement, absolutely false, and so on. They made me appear on a program on television, accepting whatever they imputed to me, which shows the brutality with which they treated me. The Army took the trouble to arrest me and the rest of my friends in order to slander our beloved organization, which was not possible since the whole Salvadoran population knows the rough methods which the government uses. Even his arguments in his defense were plain and thus weak, unsuspecting of the complex power struggles hovering over his head, the struggles which his kaleidoscopic diagrams spun out like a Van Gogh night.

He began skimming the narrative, leapfrogging with an uncanny exactness to those bits of information he needed for his records, the presence of Domingo Terrero Sanchez, a Dominican, and Julio Romero Talavera, a Costariquense, just names again, kept in solitary confinement for 550 days, 105 prisoners kept in underground prisons simply listed as missing persons, the living conditions at Mariona, 3 toilets for 500 prisoners, a spoon of beans and two tortillas for food. It was the kind of reading he was used to, but perhaps because of what the earthquake had opened up in him or perhaps because of his insistence on the reality of the platitudinous, the quotidian, the plain, he found himself halting and lingering with the flattest of Zuleta's assertions, I still have a nervous disorder and a cerebral debility, I used to lose consciousness at times, or, it is a totally depressing and beggarly life we lead, we who find ourselves as political prisoners, each one so mysterious because so indistinctive, the more evocative for lack of individuality.

When he arrived at the long peroration, Walt must have had a classical education, the sun had swung out of his window, and his reading seemed to have come full circle, for although it was filled with subjunctives, that verbal mood his American education had never trained him to quite understand, and which didn't exist at all in Chinese, I hereby authorize that anyone should publish and divulge this testimony, I hope that, let the world know that, you should know that, I ask, I ask, I call upon, let the world see the participation in all this human hunt by the government of the United States, yet all these self-references revealed not the slightest character or individual, nothing for himself, in fact a denial of self, a denial that his story had anything to do with himself, his personality, his thoughts, his history, it being nothing more than a story generated from without, by the context we all find ourselves in, so that the coherence of his story, like that of fables, what the Germans call maerchen, case histories in psychiatric handbooks or neurology books, most news accounts, found stories, myths, saints' lives, family newsletters he received at Christmas from his high-school friends, all those unaesthetic, real accounts of life, was made up by the presence of all possible other stories. They were like maps, necessarily small, necessarily abstract, necessarily schematic, useful only because they were printable, foldable, rollable, drawable on a single sheep's back, shorn of details, and thereby attaining a purely imagistic status to become a mnemonic for all the possible stories that could be played out in their spaces. So it did not matter who Walter Zuleta was, who sits in a darkened dungeon in El Salvador day after day, beaten day after day, shitting blood day after day, groaning, puking, mumbling to himself to keep his numbness and his self-pity together. Someone was there, hundreds of people were there or in the schools teaching or in small, blue apartments in Third World countries, and they all shared or would or could share the same story, their lives being what happens to them and not who they are.

When he started making entries in his files and adding diagrams to his flipbook, he was unhappy with the way he had to distribute Zuleta's account, arms dealing, Taiwan, political prisoners, etc., even though he started a new file called Walter Zuleta into which he put all private accounts. The piles of clippings were too bulky, like life, to maintain, but the system he had devised was not complex enough. He thought that perhaps one day his diagrammatic maps could be transferred to transparencies, so that one could see all the relationships at a single glance, a cartographer's vision of history. As it was, the more topics he diagrammed, the more the separate topics came together, becoming but aspects of a single topic, all relationships being massed into a single relationship. But none of this answered to some need he found to find the balance between the abstractions of history and the stories of lives. Perhaps he needed to do what Popov had done for folktales, breaking up Walter Zuleta stories into components and cross-referencing these, was it possible, into catalogues of lives, a sure blow against the illusion of individuality.

3

Standing in the little plaza of Santa Anita at dusk, he had gone back to Beto's project in late November, he tried to look inconspicuous, the beaten up gym bag where he had his camera equipment hidden tossed on the paving stones in front of him. To his right the church's low stucco wall blocked off the small orange grove where he used to wait for Beto, now filled with scaffolding and equipment for restoring the seventeenth-century parish church, though nothing had been done, he saw, since he was here last before the earthquake, the north tower still wearing its new coat of white stucco which the workmen had applied by mistake. A wedding service was going on in the small church, girls in high heels and short dresses and white gloves walked briskly across the plaza, a little late, a large family, elderly couple, the man shorter than the wife, four very stiff and serious children, came from behind the church, the church door opened, and the photographer, battery swinging, ran quickly out sidewise, found his position and snapped his flashgun at the bride and groom as they exited in the blue glow, pop, pop, pop, while people tried to squeeze past the couple to get ready to throw their fistfuls of confetti on them as they descended the stairs.

A young man stopped in front of him to watch, leaning slowly forward and then rocking back, his arms hanging limply by his side, a crumpled plastic bag in one hand, then turning towards him slowly, looked him up and down and eyed the bag, all the time rocking back and forth, finally, saying, go home, get out of here, Japanese, glue, waved his plastic bag in front of him, go away. He picked up his gym bag and headed across the plaza toward Doña Rosa's, the plaza now dark, no Beto, a small group of teenagers still barely visible in front of the health clinic sniffing glue, the truck issuing bags of water now gone.

Doña Rosa was dying of cancer, but she still held court every day from about 11 in the morning until after dark, when her husband, a butcher, came home and, sitting at the long table that connected the kitchen area with the large sitting room, waited for Doña Rosa to serve him supper while he chatted with the few lingering clients in the yellow sitting room. They had known each other since childhood, both growing up on that very block in the vacant lot slums, she a very tough and slim girl always had with her her younger brother whom she protected and brought up until he died in a construction accident at the age of eighteen, while the Sr. was always just the good man, she said. Now she was something like a borough boss: she worked in the party, attended meetings at city hall, phoned members of the governing board, knew the mayor, generally promoted the cause of the Santa Anita slums, the medical clinic in the plaza being one of her doings, and people came to her yellow cinder block living room, waited, talked of the old days, waited some more in the green plastic easy chairs, and asked for favors, and when they left, she told the others of how that one had tried to push her brother off the board walk into the mud and they got into a regular slugging and hair pulling fight, both rolling in the mud, but she beat the hell out of her, on the other side of the block by the nopal cactus, the last one in Santa Anita of all those that used to be here when she was a child and Santa Anita rural, on the other side of the big street were fields and fields of cultivated flowers. It was Doña Rosa who first suggested in her husky, disintegrating voice the article on the Santa Anita slums to Beto, who was only trying to restore the parish church for his degree in architectural restoration. When Beto finally arrived they made arrangements with Doña Rosa to work in one of the slum settlements the next morning. Without her constant presence, it was dangerous for them to walk about even in daylight.

Beto insisted they always speak Spanish in Santa Anita, it being bad enough that one of them looked Japanese and the other North American, he muttered on their way to the subway station, without attracting more attention by jabbering in a foreign language. It was a thing Beto had, being six foot two, blond and blue eyed, and brought up in Lomas and Polanco, where those traits meant power, wealth, class, but perpetual alienation from the dark masses, living and working among people for whom, he feared, he was the object of hate and fear, if not of ridicule, but as a result he was more nationalistic, more Mexican, than anybody he knew. On the other hand, Beto certainly knew better than he, because he really was just a foreigner, and when and where had he not been a foreigner, and a foreigner who had spent most his life with archival manuscripts and old maps, that being the only reason he was involved in this project anyway, to draw maps of the five slum villages grouped in Santa Anita, pretending to be a cartographer when he was really only a historian of mapmaking, so he slung his bag over his shoulder and stuck his hands in his pockets against the cold and walked on to the subway. They were out of place even if he didn't know it.

On the train he read that the Salvadoran church reported twenty people disappeared and twenty people assassinated in the past week, five of the people killed having been decapitated by the Secret Anti-Communist Army, the ESA they signed themselves, that Richard Stone, the special American representative, refused to meet with a coalition group, the FMLN and the FDR, opposed to the Salvadoran government, because he insisted that he was a neutral mediator while the opposition group insisted that he represented the American side in the conflict, and that the Arch-bishop of San Salvador, Monseñor Arturo Rivera y Damas said, dialogue is blocked when one of the parties refuses to listen to the arguments of the other, when one of the parties pretends to be the sole mediator and dispenser of justice.

The next morning, with kids following him around the dirt paths calling kungfu, bizarre because Beto really was a master at it and had competed internationally, he photographed and measured and took elevations and laid out angles, drew diagrams and sketches all morning, while Beto talked to women, arms crossed or doing laundry, flipped a peso coin across his knuckles from one finger to the next for the kids, was led to water spigots, nodding while men recounted their complaints, all staring uncomfortably at the faucet.

In Santa Anita there were five lost cities, which is what they were called in Mexico, barriadas in Lima and Bogota, ranchos or ranchitos in Caracas, favellas in Rio, a common history, each with its different qualities, one fairly new, one as old as thirty or forty years, all built on vacant lots and maintained by squatters' rights, though he was surprised that people paid rent, not to the legal owners of the lots but to individuals who had somehow laid claim to some small section and by force of a mysterious hierarchy demanded and received rent on houses built on that section, the rents sometimes being as high as rents on new apartments in high-rises in Polanco.

The people built with an amazing assortment of materials, from cardboard and flattened tin cans to metal advertising signs, to rubble, concrete blocks, plastic sheets, steel plates, brick, to sturdy two-inch thick planks, one shack being entirely held together by lag bolts. The huts leaned on one another, sharing walls and roofs, and were crisscrossed with clotheslines and electrical wires, and now that the rains had gone, they were very beautiful, the variety of textures and colors offset by innumerable flowers in pots hanging on the walls and in the window sills and just as many bird cages hanging under the eaves.

The city had provided a water spigot for about every seventy to a hundred people, but of course after the earthquake the water stopped flowing, and each lost city had a sewer pipe, over which in one the people had built a line of five communal toilets, flushed with buckets of wash water, but in another the sewer pipe was simply an open-ended pipe surrounded by a sheet of corrugated tin. They stole their electricity by means of hot wires from the utility poles in the streets, which was understood as a form of public philanthropy by the state-owned electric company, one of the benefits of living under a government that advertised itself as socialist. The people seemed able to live with their situation, making more or less of it according to their energies. In one of the settlements, the paths were being paved. In another, the people as a whole had refused to pay rent and were tensely waiting for something nasty to happen. In some houses, they had managed running water and toilets. In the one where Beto had brought him to talk to the owner, there was a shower, the only one in all the lost cities.

He had a thick manila envelope on the dark, scrubbed and oiled table, and at first it was hard to see his face, because the four of them sitting around the table so filled the small, low- ceilinged room with its one tiny window that they seemed to have pushed out the light and with it the raucous noise of the children. The house was the second oldest in the lost city, about forty years old: Sr. Muñoz had built it himself in stages, of course, though there were houses in the neighborhood that were built half-professionally, he meant commercially, in order to be rented rather than for oneself, this room was the first part, and it had been rebuilt, like the roof, several times, but the problem of rebuilding for many people was that it raised the value of the dwelling so that the pseudo-landlords then asked for more money: in fact the pseudo-landlords were their main problem, remembering the two men who had driven up when he was trying to get a panorama photograph of the lost city asking who had given him permission to do that and saved by Doña Rosa he had ducked out of the altercation. There were many special ways the neighbors were bound together, for example the tandas, communal savings clubs, each family putting into a kitty a small amount of money a week and each family taking turns weekly spending the money, which were traditional among the poor, but the major impetus drawing them together had been Cristo Feren, it sounded like. Cristo Something organized them against the landlords, taught them politics, initiated their communal building projects, told jokes in good street style, made them elect officers, follow certain rules about drugs and health, start a teen club, he was revered as a god, even though he seemed to have been pretty young, but he lived here in the ghetto, with us, brought his family, a nice quiet girl whose name he had forgotten but which Doña Rosa remembered, Marta, and two small children, Carlito and Sung, they threatened him, they asked him to leave the country, took his papers from him. He was losing the conversation, you mean he wasn't Mexican, Cristo Feren was North American, so what happened to him, he disappeared, you mean he went back to the US, no, they didn't mean that, of course, only a naive American would miss the irony of that word, and he, who had files on this topic, over three hundred disappeared people in Mexico, should have known better, so he disappeared and left only this book.

Sr. Muñoz took a typescript out of the envelope and laid it in front of him, the title page a bit smeared and not quite flat, the corners ruffled, *Cartas de Plymouth,* Letters from Plymouth, by Christopher Ng, good grief, that was it, how could he miss that name, he's Chinese, no, Chinese-American like you, no, no, I'm Chinese, but it was true, he was very American, he had a '32 Ford Sedan when he was in high school with a '48 flathead V-8 Mercury engine, a tomato crate for the driver's seat, he slouched and dragged his heels when he walked, and his speech was cluttered with diphthongs, slurs, swallowed consonants, blends, so that he couldn't even recognize a Chinese name when he heard it, but was his wife also Chinese, no, she was gringa, like Carol. They did not know how Christopher came to Santa Anita, a few years ago some gringo evangelicals had tried to move into the neighborhood, they were not well received, lived in a bus for a few weeks and left, Christopher may have been at the university at one time, he got along well with everyone, only the landlords hated him, that was three years ago, they try to keep fighting, they have not forgotten the things Christopher taught them, but they needed help still, the article Beto and he were to write would help, he could not lend him the manuscript to read because it was the only memory he had of Christopher but he was welcomed to come here anytime to read it, perhaps Sr. Muñoz would go with him to a copy center to xerox it, perhaps.

Rocking and swaying on the subway home, he read another narration from El Salvador, this one taken by the lawyer Marianella Garcia Villas, the president of the Salvadoran Commission on Human Rights just before she was arrested and killed by the Army. He would call her Walter Zuleta in his files, as he would call the anonymous person who gave her the declaration. She had been gathering evidence of the Army's use of chemical weapons after denials by American advisors in the field with the Salvadoran Army, flying reconnaissance for them, he remembered from another article. Somewhere in the Department of Chalatenango, at 11 o'clock in the morning of the third day of October 1985, I, Walter Zuleta, he read, 25 years old, a nurse living in the canton of La Cruz, declare that on Saturday, the 19th of September, we, a civil population, were attacked by the Army. About four in the afternoon, they were attacked by planes firing rockets and dropping bombs, two A-37's, a small plane flying reconnaissance, a helicopter machine-gunning. Also, 90 mm mortars were fired at us. Because of these circumstances we were moved to a place called Palo Grande. He loved it, the narrative so sparse and schematic, the character so anonymous and abstract, like the other Zuleta, like this guy Christopher, like earthquake victims, figures caught in action that was beyond themselves, who they were or what aspect of individual personality or thought they possessed having nothing to do with their fate, brought into life and given humanity by the event, peripheral figures in someone else's story, no Greek tragic heros dragging out their own character lines, but just a simple we were moved to a place called Big Tree. His thoughts, too, and his past and his habits and his tastes, his very sense of himself, may have nothing to do with his life: that seemed to have been true for Christopher. Perhaps, his maps would cause his own story to disappear, and he would find an entrance into history.

About 150 of them were on foot, the children unable to stay on their feet, crying, and being forced by their mothers to keep walking though they cried because they knew the enemy was near and wanted to kill us. We arrived at Palo Grande. There we took refuge, but a light plane flew over us, as if trying to make sure exactly where we were. Frequently, the first plane flies over us to see where we are. Then other planes come to bomb us. In this case, it was decided to move to Tenango. The following day, at about 11 in the morning, that attack came. We succeeded in getting out, but when we were passing along the edge of the river, the enemy started to fire mortars at the whole fleeing population, and at the same time, the planes were machine-gunning us. The napalm and white phosphorous bombs started falling, burning the children and the old people. The mothers were left with second and third degree burns. I was trying to help them when a rocket exploded nearby, wounding my daughter, and I was also hurt. At this place about 175 people were killed, he read. The emptiness hypnotized him, made the narrative susceptible to his reading mind, no character or plot imposing themselves on either the story or his imagination, as might in a piece of fiction, as if held by the puzzle of reality that constantly eluded him, so that even in the midst of the story's terror, he took pleasure in its emptiness.

The burns from the napalm bombs left enormous white blisters. I was burned on the side of my leg. My daughter's burns began to change color and became purple. Later the whole leg got hard and turned purple. The leg gave off a terrible stink, and as a consequence of the burns, she passed away, since we had no medicine. Laconic and horrifying, he thought. He noticed that where she was wounded, it had gotten full of puss almost immediately. This happened on the 23rd of September.

The closing statement, as in all the Zuleta narratives, offered the document to public use, use this testimony as is fitting, appropriately denying private ownership in the statement and, seemingly, in the experience related, too, here comes everybody.

4

In the morning he collated the news articles from the previous day. A study by the United Nations that showed that one hundred ninety pharmaceutical products classified as dangerous and either withdrawn from the market or severely restricted in the US and in Europe were being sold in Latin America by American and European companies had to be cross-referenced with the information from the Mexican Minister of Finance that in recent talks in Washington over Mexico's problem with debts the first order of business brought up by the American President was the opening up of the Mexican market for more American pharmaceuticals. In Nicaragua, the contras continued their campaign against civilians, the number of children under twelve killed by the contras rose to 134 for the year, the total number of civilian casualties for only two months reached 600, including the execution of 29 telephone operators who had volunteered to harvest coffee in San Juan del Rio Coco. The Israeli government reopened its Embassy in San Salvador after the visit of the Israeli Minister of Defense. Israel is already the major supplier of weapons in Guatemala and in Honduras is second to the US in military aid. It did not seem difficult to imagine a Walter Zuleta whose everyday story touched on all these points.

In the afternoon, he returned to the Muñoz house to read Christopher's manuscript, April 3, 1982, January 16, 1982, Dear Harry, January 3, 1982, he flipped through it, bla bla bla, September 10, 1981, historians think change is something, but things become different without any change at all, Dear Abe, August 1, 1981, Hi

Tom, Dear Jack, the supremacy of money, as his eyes grew more used to the darkness, thirty-five dated letters addressed to different people, friends or American Presidents or friends with the names of the Presidents, he wondered, beginning July 4, 1981, Dear George, Martha, mine not thine, says I can't talk to Americans, but I can, it's just that you can't understand me since I stopped being American, but then since you've stopped being American, too, in a sense, I'll try explaining to you what happened, I've become Xipe-Totec. You probably don't know Xipe-Totec, he did, the Mexican god of revival, spring rains, sacrifice, a chubby cheeked boy you can never see because his eyes looked out from within the flayed skin of a man, god of metals, too, and like his related entity, Hurricane, a drunkard, sometimes wearing a coat that looked as if fashioned from feathers but was really of raindrops, sometimes hobbling on one leg, some places lying on his back with his legs doubled over where he had fallen, looking astonished and indistinguishable from the chac mool, whom he might have been, or perhaps he was just another consequence of Tlaloc. So Christopher was another, but self-conscious, Walter Zuleta and one who knew his own identity was anonymous and changeable and thus universal and mythic, knowing that names, personal history, individuality covered and suppressed a more real, more fluid world of figurative relations, so maybe he should rename all his Walters Christopher, a Chinese-American-Mexican god, terrific.

I needed a new skin, he continued, not the trite snakeskin idea, but someone else's skin, the skin of some poor, hollow-cheeked bastard flayed alive by the gods of reality while he kicked and screamed in self-pity and anger, and don't think that it's the yellow skin that I want to get rid of. It's the whitey in me that I can't stand or rather the American in me, but maybe it's the same thing. Martha seemed to have been right, since Washington, of all people, certainly would not have understood him. Washington had probably never seen a Chinese, though there was one living in central Boston at that time, so perhaps Washington's ideas had to be reconsidered with this in mind, as one of his friends, an art historian, told him that all of

Joshua Reynolds' art theory had to be reconsidered on the basis that he only knew Italian painting through fakes and forgeries. He was tired of living in American cliches, say no to drugs, a woman should have some say over what happens to her own body, American style democracy, it's time to pay attention to the victims of crime, tired of emotions lived within the range of soap-opera relations, just as tired of American excesses, but mostly tired of American lack of self-criticism. If I say to an American all those things, he thinks they're my pet peeves, if I say that America's a fucking capitalistic imperialistic war-mongering country, he thinks I'm complaining about the government or about the corporations or about the military. He doesn't get that I don't like him, him because he is the culture, because the culture, all of it, the government, the corporations, the military, is in him, in the people, and if finally he gets it, he just resents it, who let you in here anyway. And, he surely never gets that I mean myself, too. He might take a step back and say, Americans haven't liked themselves for a long time, and he might sympathize and agree that something ought to be done or he might argue that things aren't what they use to be or he might say that I'm full of shit or he might say, so what's new, everybody knows that, give us something fresh, or he might say that I should revel in it, go with the flow, baby, but he just doesn't get it.

And, I blame you for it, George, for your making of a nation and not letting all the different kinds of people, the variety of the masses, have this land, for your repeated warnings about foreign powers that defined a them from an us, like drawing boundaries in the mind that left us all paranoid and needing a patriotism I don't want, for exploiting the myth of the melting pot, the myth of new beginnings, for annihilating the past so that we can have no guilt, no past so that every fault we might find in ourselves could be passed on, blamed on the old world, with the creation of this new nation in this new world, and woe to the natives whose presence denied that it was a new world, this Eden with every Adam a self-made man, blame you personally, mythically, individually and figuratively, allegorically and metaphorically and historically for not letting Americans see the old world in themselves, for not giving us the chance to see ourselves and to come to terms with ourselves but only to delude ourselves. If you could only see the situation from my point of view, you'd see how absurd and incomprehensible, how tragic and comic, it is for me, who should be Chinese, to call you my founding father. How did I get a wasp for a father?

The Zapotecs, he read, say, niru zazalu' guira'xixe neza guidxilayu' ti ganda guidxelu' lii, which means that you have to walk the paths of all the pueblos of earth before you meet your real self. He took that to imply, borrowing an image his namesake used for the geographical world, unde spericus sperica spericum idest rotundus & solidus ad modum spere, that the spiritual world was round and that only by going all the way around that world can we find ourselves, and that if we think we know ourselves, it is only an illusion, because the self which is real is the other side of the person we think we are, though by the time we've walked all the paths we may have put on so many selves we would not know who is meeting whom.

So, George, there is no escaping it, there's no criticism, of self or of the culture, without this little jaunt. I'm here in this new, new Plymouth, Xipe-Totec beginning another cycle of history, a rejection, a landing, a renewal of myself and of America. When he finished, he might have looked up from the pale blue Brother typewriter he had gotten at the piety mountain, his only luxury, to see Martha sitting startlingly close across the small table, her head bent over a pile of papers she was correcting, tapping the pencil in her right hand slowly on the oil-spotted bare wood, one end and then the other. Her light brown hair was pulled back behind her head, and in her print dress, the longish Salvation Army kind she always wore, even here in Santa Anita when he dressed in dungarees and knit shirts like everyone else, she looked more like a Walker Evans photograph than a belated hippy, which she thought she was. Around the room, above and below them, the darkness sucked away the light from the unfrosted bulb over the table, and in the barely lit corner behind Martha he saw the kids sleeping, sprawled on the double bed that formed a T with their bed.

He wondered if it was true, no cultural criticism without self-criticism: is that what he was doing with his charts of American and European world actions, pursuing something that had no basis because he had not the self-awareness to understand the relationships he found, that had no value because no one, at least no American, had freed himself enough from his identity to appreciate them. His colleagues would not take his charts to be history or reality, just politics and so boring, so it seemed to him that somehow Christopher's problem turned out to be his also. He wondered who Christopher imagined as his audience anyway: did he think of his letters as public or private expiation, writing in Spanish gave him, presumably, a non-American audience, if he thought of those things, could he have imagined that a Chinese would read the letters, perhaps the only person who could understand him, did he mean him to read them, and he wondered who Christopher was, where he came from, he knew so few Chinese-Americans who were politically conscious and these were sure enough of their Americaness to question their Chineseness but not sure enough of their Chineseness to question the American in them. Euro-Chinese were different: he knew at least two cases, a brilliant girl close to the radical student movement in Germany, she was brought up in England, France, and Germany, and she died of an infection in Shanghai, and a friend of his in graduate school, brought up in England and France, who returned to China to work for the revolution, but Christopher was American, though he obviously did not like being one, what had turned him, what had happened to him?

Sr. Muñoz told him that Christopher taught English for money, giving business executives private lessons in their offices, while his wife corrected papers at an institute for translators and interpreters, that was on Rio Tiber only a block away from his apartment, he had even seen her on the streets, a blonde girl wearing clogs and a depression era dress, or was his memory an aberration? The whole family had disappeared, no one even knew how, they were gone, and then some men came to the house, we all watched, and they took everything away.

He turned to March 15, 1982, Dear Andy, the people in this new world are small and delicate, fine boned and warm skinned, and they move among themselves with grace and incredible courtesy, but I'm like you taught me to be, all American lunker, bulging pectorals when young, bulging paunch when middle-aged, and bulging prostate when old, vulgar, uncouth, totally uncomfortable with courtesy and politeness, and I'm still American enough to like it. My impoliteness gives me a special positive feeling of pleasure, a jouissance the Frenchies call it, I know you don't like foreign things, but you'll like this, Andy, because it means playing like a cat with a mouse or like a horse-soldier with an Indian, it means impoliteness is full of power, there's a pride in it, and knowledge and familiarity, it means being impolite stands for equalitarianism and independence and a kind of American superiority. And there's a swagger to it, like I know how to talk man to man, brother to brother, standing up together against all that upperclass bullshit, so that when I'm impolite I'm telling the American success story, the rise of the working classes, a frontier story as well as a factory story. My jouissance is filled with these stories of independence, self- sufficiency, and personal attainment that make up American individualism, so my impoliteness, our impoliteness, shouts to the world that we in America are vigorous, energetic, efficient as steam engines, and aggressive, because if I refuse to be polite I can violate the other person's own integrity by giving him existence only in my world and in terms of my interests, asserting myself and my priority, I depreciate others. I still take jouissance in attacking social behavior, conventionality, codes, rules, decorum and other inhibiting artificialities, I still assert the validity of self over all external forms, even though I know impoliteness is a private version of imperialism and terrorism and habitual politeness is peaceful waters. What you taught me, Andy, persists like an accent, I still hear the disdain in my Buenos dias, señora, as I hear my flat American accent, and he heard it, too, imbedded in the style of Christopher's writing, that strange nasal flatness which all Chinese-Americans had no matter how native their English, resonating out of some peculiarly Chinese bone structure in their sinus passages, like his own dull, uneventful voice. When I can speak rapidly with that energy and crispness Mexican Spanish has, I'll carry in the subjunctive of my Que vaya bien something unAmerican and human.

It was clearly a demonic exorcism, but did it work, could it work, and if it worked, what would he be when no longer an American?

5

He found no trace of Christopher, Martha, and their children, at the University or in the intellectual circles, no dissertation registered in the US, no publications listed in the periodical indices. At the school for interpreters and translators, he found that Martha had only done piece work, picking up papers to correct every now and then without any formal association. They knew nothing about her other than that she had presented an American degree, forgotten where, and could correct English grammar. From what Sr. Muñoz had told him about Christopher's organizing tactics, he recognized elements of the SDS, but he was too young to have been in the movement, and in any case his aim seemed entirely private rather than political, though his thinking was all political and though political action was his method of expiation. So, unlike the other anonymous Walters, aka Christophers, this Christopher did not even have the solidity of a story, being simply a kind of absence, even the letters lacking some center of identity, jumping from topic to topic and style to style like a brain damaged Luria patient, copying out, sometimes plagiarizing, whole passages from his eclectic readings, unscholarly, uncertain of his facts yet assertive of his opinions, haranguing and badgering his personal demon by always finding him at the origin of his culture's faults, but feeling severed from the academic world by his present pursuits, he sympathized with Christopher's lack of direction or method. Perhaps, he thought, Christopher's invisibility in these letters symbolized his lack of identity in white America, a quiet minority they call us, or his intent in Mexico to shed that identity or, again, symbolized his fate, an appropriate historical irony, as a disappeared person.

In his striped lawnchair in front of the picture window, almost no signs left of an earthquake though no one knew how many lives it had ended or changed, he read the letters to the Presidents through a second time. From some small event in his daily life, today I bought a sieve at the supermarket, picking it out and paying for it without knowing or learning what it is called in Spanish, he extrapolated cultural criticism, that the history of marketing and production favored a general disarticulation in the society, the supermarket being contrasted with bartering, bartering gives me the feeling that I am near some originary moment when the object has just come into being and is still free of its commercial value, where the object has not yet become the expression of greed, not yet encumbered and entangled in the mercantile network, the uncertainty over the price being a kind of virginity. This disarticulation was accompanied by a narrowing of the people's social activity, people no longer need to ask nor offer help, information, interact, exchange values, wisdom, and not needing to talk about these things, they no longer need to know anything, accompanied as well by a loss of their ability to express complex ideas of morality or politics.

He argued that Americans deliberately invented patriotism to trivialize freedom so that the revolutionary fervor would be dispelled, any country founded on revolution could be destroyed by revolution, and a similar fear lay behind the standing army and the enormously well developed road and transport system, no place to hide in America. Americans truly believed that freedom is living out one's desire rather than the chance to act with a clear conscience, yes, do your own thing, Jack, moral choice, he once saw in a serious journal of social work, being described as the choice to buy an airline ticket from several companies. Desire, which sums up gluttony, lechery, avarice, envy, pride, and spiritual thirst, six of the seven deadly sins in our fallen language, the seventh being what happens when desire is thwarted, is America, generating its whole economic and political history, determining everyone's lives, a land of enormous, gigantic, monumental desire, and since by definition wanting is not having, the pursuit of happiness is an eternal agony of anger, and so Americans pout and gripe and blame and abuse and fight and play and make love furious with the world.

For Christopher, every aspect of the present pointed to some mistake in the past, it was all wrong from the beginning. Reason can never cope with desire, so American democracy, an ideal of rationalism, can never cope with the forms of power desire created in the nineteenth and twentieth centuries, those corporate power structures, clearly hierarchical rather than democratic, outside the structures of democracy, beyond the voting power of the people, so having the right to vote could not guarantee social equality and power to the people, this, in addition to the inability of the people to exercise truly moral choices given their lack of information and an educational system that promoted the ideology that this was the best of all possible worlds, made suffrage not only superfluous, which is why the last President was elected by 27% of the people, but, viewed cynically, a sop given the people by the government in order to satisfy their delusions.

He returned to eighteenth-century rationalism to find there the roots of American racism and again to point out its inadequate theory of mind and imagination, pre-Kantian as well as pre-Freudian, and again to show its relation to American optimism and American pride and American naivete, all attributes he considered dangerous when coupled to American power. He saw the concept of individualism as an aberration made up not only of Reformation theology but of criminal ethics, a legacy of Hakluyt's call to people the new world with Englishmen who had lost their money and self-respect, imprisoned debtors, ex-soldiers, children of wandering beggars, and valiant youths rusting and hurtful by lack of employment, a desperate, suspicious group of individuals, a legacy added to by eighteenth-century English bond servants, and argued, as he himself had argued in his own mind, that private thoughts and feelings upon which we base our sense of selves are in fact shareable and shared, independent of our physical entities or identities, formed by histories of social behavior and social psychology and language, so that culture is the actual organism of life within which we are only lifeless physical atoms.

Many of the ideas and opinions were neither radical nor new, Christopher often rehashing social criticism of the thirties, probably without even knowing it, but they were meditative and haunted by the reality of his story, a totally unknown story, but certainly as real as any of the other Christopher stories, so these ideas had a fleshiness as ideas committed to and lived out. It was pretty simple, Christopher wanted to know why Americans were so bad, and he pursued the answer speculatively and at random, while he, what had he done, had avoided the question, though not really, for the question was there in all his charts, only he followed by habit a research method that hid moral imperatives behind a seeming objectivity of relationships. He was like a modern cartographer, schematizing to show relations, while Christopher was an ancient mapmaker trying to represent the whole landscape, the shadows and the forms of land as well as the distances. They were not that different, a politicized street intellectual and an academic historian. If the Walter stories were a narrative version of his abstract maps, peopling their space, then these letters were the settings for those realities. In fact, when he thought of that equation a little, it occurred to him that the letters were empty just like the Walter stories or his maps, communal because they were empty, the elements all trite and commonplace but entirely open to the imagination. If he were Christopher, he would speculate that all the business in scholarship about originality, fresh ideas, all that time spent identifying so-and-so's ideas and so-and-so's distinctive methods, so-and-so's inventive terms, was a colossal misunderstanding leading simply to the commercial business of scholarship and eventually to a great deal of pain, for he remembered the humiliating calm of the faculty meeting two years ago when a colleague was forced to admit haltingly in front of them all that several sentences in his recently published book were plagiarized. Historians should know better, this propertizing of ideas and language being a very recent, capitalistic development in Europe and America, not at all a problem in Classical or Renaissance cultures, and in China, the whole conservatism of the culture was founded on the rectitude and propriety of copying, forgery, and plagiarism, signs of the wholeness of the culture, the communality of its intellectual world, recognition that language and ideas originate and are understood in the group, in the culture. He decided to fill his next book with plagiarisms, just to make the point that ideas, like people, were all commonplace, a good topographic metaphor.

He returned to his reading. Did you hear, Thomas, that they shot and killed a man in Utah who resisted sending his children to public school, a mortal sin apparently and so demonstrative of your stated constitutional will to form a more and more perfect union by reaching into the daily lives of the people, a will and a reach made more terrible by the money, technology, communications, efficiency, and practicality an industrial, capitalistic system furnishes the state. And you've succeeded, no union is more uniform with its codes and regulations and minimum specifications and ratings and professional standards and qualifications. We have come to Tocqueville's nightmare for which he said there was as yet no name, a democracy that he described as covering the whole of social life with a network of petty, complicated rules that are both minute and uniform, not breaking men's will, but softening, bending, and guiding it, seldom enjoining, but often inhibiting, action, not destroying anything, but preventing much from being born, not at all tyrannical, yet hindering, restraining, enervating, stifling, and stultifying so much that in the end the nation is no more than a flock of timid and hardworking animals with the government as its shepherd, each individual withdrawn into himself, almost unaware of the fate of others, the whole world for him straitened into his family and his personal friends. Did you envision that, Thomas, that it took only two hundred years for American schools to destroy thousands of years of European wisdom and thought? Did you know, Thomas, that life in Taiwan and Singapore is chaotic, open, and free, perhaps as antidotes to repression, so that I equate dictatorship with freedom and democracy with control, though the real issue is the state's will and power. He should tell Christopher about Kafka's image of the Chinese Emperor, so distant from his scattered subjects that he was like the evaporating idea of infinity itself to them, an image of chaos in tyranny not different from the description given by the first Portuguese sailors shipwrecked in Southern China, who, taken captive and sent off north to the Emperor, wandered around China for years like a band of beggars asking their way and being sent hither and thither, sometimes also asking the name of the country they were in and being told the country had no name.

Christopher always looked for origins, processes whereby things became the way they were, so he distrusted everything American, for being American, for having come out of some racist, power hungry, greedy, imperialist, platitudinous, hypocritical crevice in the American character, distrusted Martha's feminism for its dependency on issues of money, distrusted his own involvement in the ecological movement because its fondness for wilderness could not be separated from the edenic dream that caused so much destruction in America, distrusted the American school system as a propaganda machine, distrusted colleges and universities because, somehow, he found that the earliest charters were granted purely on the basis of financial considerations, distrusted American games, American inventions, American songs, American stories, American forms of all kinds, and believed that every form had the potential if not the efficient aim to be an instrument of American hegemony.

Christopher stated all his opinions with certainty, yet the bravura was pathetic, because he always knew that no one was listening. He was listening, but then he was Chinese, so it didn't do much good, or did he listen with an American ear, was that the question, finally, whether he would choose to be Chinese or American? It doesn't matter, does it Cal, because you're free if you feel you are, so who am I to tell you you're not free, and as long as Americans aren't too good on morality, and what do they have to be moral about, they can get their freedom feelies by just beating the shit out of some other country, after Vietnam, everybody had better watch out.

And, it doesn't matter, he thought about his charts of American foreign policy, not to Americans, but it mattered to everyone else who was not American, because Americans not being morally free, American power was raw and undirected, like a seven-headed dragon. All that purely physical power, consuming light and food, beer, steaks, milk, pizzas, heat and electricity, gas and oil, coal, wood, chemicals and speed and fission and fusion to make work in the physical world, turned out to be a metaphor for the human world, so that the more energy Americans eat, the more the great beast threatens every person in the world, threatens him with physical annihilation, economic ruin, social degradation, spiritual loss, moral shame, and cultural dissipation, because the multitudes of all the nations are the mountains she feeds on and she, the flesh they eat. Every Walter and every Christopher is subject to her actions, so that this Babylon is the single greatest impediment to world freedom. Every small ripple of her heavy folds changes instantly, marvels of the electronic world, the buying and selling in every country of money and gold and silver, precious stones, pearls and fine linen, purple, silk and scarlet, of thyine wood, ivory bowls, brass, iron, marble, cinnamon, perfumes, ointments, wine, oil, fine flour and wheat, sheep, pigs, horses, chariots and slaves and souls of men. Not unlike the situation of the American colonists in the eighteenth century, most people in the world are at the mercy of a foreign and apparently arbitrary power in whose governing they have no say. American power is not always threatening, not always felt or decried, but it's always there and, comparatively, is always staggering, 43 battleships and 4 carriers off the coasts of little Nicaragua, a budget deficit so large that the mind of man cannot imagine it any more than it can imagine infinity, 40,000 nuclear targets in the Soviet Union, enough to destroy each city a hundred times over, and being so great and being always present, the threat will eventually be actualized, for the nature of the beast is centripetal, accumulating and adhering power to itself blindly, ignorant and careless of its extensions, so the colonist, who lives with no liberty or dignity, will eventually be victimized unjustly, cruelly, arbitrarily, simply because Americans feel free. Being so concentrated, America's needs, real and imagined, and a large animal has a large imagination, are many, and so its net of self-protection, which it calls self-interest, is extensive, ubiquitous, and its everywhere colonies become the places where its gigantic paranoia is acted out. In Namibia the United States supplies South African troops, 100,000 of them, one soldier to every five Namibian citizens, in order to secure itself against the threat of Angola, while incidentally maintaining control of the uranium mines that supply one quarter of the ore imported by the United States, Great Britain, France, and West Germany. Give me your tired, your poor, your huddled masses and I'll turn them into pasty-faced, hectoring technocrats.

He could feel the sarcasm bubble up as phrases, someone else's phrases, phrases he could read, apprehend, seize upon, but as if not his own, and he was surprised at the indignation, being unused to anger, generally too remote to find himself in altercations, but also because he thought of his project intellectually, as cool history rather than hot politics, which was why he appreciated the commonplaces of Christopher's ideas, old stories repeated made history, new ideas were just aberrations, but he recognized his anger as peculiarly American, righteous indignation, good guys against the bastards, in fact the most telling part of Christopher's own demon, inseparable from his American self-certainty and his also very American grumbling dissatisfaction that energized his quest. So, in some hidden seam of his fabric this American worm had quiesced until drawn out, ironically, by the heat of Christopher's anti-American self-flagellations, and if that were so, how could he stand with the placid, anger-free Walter Zuletas of this world, neither he nor Christopher, unless it were possible to be victim and victimizer at the same time.

6

Sitting in the stony silence of the National Archives where he had come every day the year before to look at the extraordinary land claim maps of the colonial period, half maps and half paintings, their primitive handling of spatial representation suggesting a kind of missing link in the history of European cartography, a link he sought between Ptolemaic geography and Renaissance painting with its full use of perspective, he could not help feeling the enormous gap between then and now. He had returned that day to peruse the Mexican diplomatic dispatches from Shanghai for 1942 which Christopher claimed showed that the US not only knew, as indeed the whole diplomatic corp in China knew, that Pearl Harbor would be bombed but had partially engineered the attack by preparing to make the first strike against Japan if the Japanese did not attack Pearl Harbor before the monsoons, the Mexican consul indicating that the war with Japan was for many years the aim of US policy in China for reasons both mercantile and racist and that though Mexico had to side with her ally to the north for political reasons, for reasons of justice and racial solidarity, she had to sympathize with the Japanese, though it was certain the US would try to perpetrate the schoolbook myth of the dastardly secret Japanese attack. The dispatch was as Christopher said, and Christopher was probably right that the more cars Japan sells the deeper the myth will burrow, but he did not know what it all meant, though he was certain that whatever it meant, it had something to do with him, his parents' decision to emigrate from China to escape the war, with his Chineseness or with his Americaness, with his mapping of US history, with his descent from a professional historian into a street intellectual, with the fact that having lost all sense of objectivity, a Swiss cheese kind of open-mindedness, unable to balance the multifarious and contradictory facets of history, he no longer had a home in the academy, so that whatever it meant, it would have to be entered into his maps, which were turning autobiographic in the same way as Christopher's history.

He had spent the past week redrawing his maps, starting with a set just on recent Latin American events. At the center of each radial map was a single event, and splaying out from that center, in red for before and in blue for after, were the other events coincident to it, the distance from the central event measured by a product of time and logical closeness, the angular position determined by sixty topics, oil prices, economic aid, foodstuffs, military intervention, communications, cultural exchange, banking, statistics, ecology, pharmaceutical markets, vegetable oil, rubber, political parties, and on, grouped according to the quadrants of relationships, formal, material, methodological, and ideological, and so mapped, the curious coincidences of daily events in the world no longer looked like serendipitous quirks of his fantasy and memory, no longer even like giant conspiracies whispered in the darkness of his paranoia but became the certain patterns of history. Hanging about the walls of the apartment, pushing out Carol's and Rihan's drawings, these blue and red maps whirling about black centers documented that every White House certification of a human rights improvement in El Salvador followed reports from news sources, from the Archbishopric of San Salvador, and from the US Embassy itself that the situation had declined, our side beating the other guys by a ratio of 30 to 1 in political killings of civilians, murders by the army, disappearances, so that such knowing lying, knowing not only that it was lying but knowing that everyone knew it was a lie, could only be a cynical performance played out before an equally cynical audience, a perfect display of representative government.

The maps documented, too, that the official US figures for trade between Mexico and the US differed by tens of billions of dollars, by as much as thirty percent, every year from the Mexican figures, so that the political decisions as to import and export duties, quotas, embargoes could be given a statistical basis, which, however, was highly inaccurate or maybe even fictitious, and when in 1982 the US government needed to claim a deficit so as to put economic pressures on Mexico for its attempt to participate in the Contadora agreements, the figures showed this deficit.

They narrated that between 1979 and 1983, 4.5 billion dollars were transferred from Central America to American banks, the earnings from which must have been about 500 million dollars a year to the advantage of the American economy, far more than the money given the Central American countries in aid, which mostly never got into the Central American economies anyway since it was spent buying American weapons and supplies, so that foreign aid rarely left the US, though it left the working class, since the maps schematized the economics of the Central American policy as lower and middle class American tax dollars being given to the upper classes of Central America in order to allow them to invest in the American economy where the arms industry and the business community were able to share in the benefits, a common story according to his maps, the upward mobility of money. The same end result could be achieved by simply distributing the money among the arms manufacturers, with a great deal less bloodshed and suffering, but then the US would have to allow other nations to determine their own futures.

The maps told the combined guerrilla forces in El Salvador at between 6,000 and 7,000, for the eradication of which the US paid $13,000 per guerrilla per year and El Salvador paid about 8,000 deaths of non-guerrillas per year.

But all the maps were themselves satellites of a single sun, the 1984 Contadora agreement between Venezuela, Panama, Mexico, and Colombia, ostensibly a plan to negotiate peace in Central America but actually a message directed at the US declaring Latin American independence from the American imperium, a message immediately understood in Washington think tanks, and in fact, long prepared for, thus producing the immediate American attempt to create a second sun, Nicaragua, for shifting the focus from El Salvador to Nicaragua meant shifting from a defensive position in El Salvador to an offensive strategy, because using Nicaragua as its pawn against Contadora allowed the US to work against Contadora while claiming to work for peace, because a victory in Nicaragua would demonstrate to Contadora nations that Central America and thus Latin America on the whole was still within the American sphere of influence, and so, around this artificial second sun, this poor, beleaguered Nicaragua, spiralled the daily charades of American policy. We do more than one thing at a time, said the Secretary of State, and we do, playing good cop/bad cop, disorienting, offering peace with one hand, slapping with the other, hectoring, accusing, badgering, appointing Nicaragua's most outspoken enemies to negotiate with Nicaragua, starving and terrorizing the peasants so they will run riot, daily leaking news of a possible invasion, but the enemy is the Contadora nations, and so about the first sun, the real sun, the US launched, as planetary events against Venezuela, Mexico, Panama, and Colombia, the oil price squeeze, helps the oil situation anyway, launched the drug war, good for diverting attention from the growing anti-nuclear movement, restricted imports and raised interest rates, a rise of 1% costing Latin countries $1,000,000,000 to $1,500,000,000 a year in interest payments, incidentally allowing an enormous increase in spending at home, tripling the debt to stockpile military equipment for twenty years into the next millenniu. And, if this doesn't work, we can always invade, Panama being a good choice since we had to give the canal back to them and the IRS is damned tired of people hiding their money in banks there.

Further maps focused on actions to destabilize Central American countries to make Contadora negotiations more difficult, relating the buying of Honduras, business is business, the best client makes the best friend, said the Honduran President's spokesman when describing the American request to participate in a covert war against Nicaragua, relating that to establishing an arms industry and green beret training camps for Costa Rica, a country which didn't have or want an army, a favorite story narrating the CIA purchase of an estate near the Nicaraguan border called the Bat which used to belong to the Somoza family to use as a training camp to teach the local gendarmes how to hang up prisoners in wire cages for interrogation, relating these actions to the use of Israeli, Taiwanese, Korean, and Argentinean middlemen in Honduras, El Salvador, and Guatemala to make Central America appear an international problem, and relating these to the coup in Guatemala to oust the pro-Contadora President, one of his favorite concatenations in which the maps began truly to narrate, allowing him to see around the lives of the people involuted: an unknown American seen in the presidential palace in Guatemala City with a walkie-talkie at the moment of the military take-over turned up two months later in Portland, Oregon, as Christopher Dove, former aid in the American Embassy in Guatemala, speaking to the Lions Club luncheon, I'm not much of a public speaker, but I'm pleased to be here this afternoon to share with you my experiences as a hands-on participant in our country's foreign policy, claiming the coup in Guatemala as a new style of American diplomacy, claiming his eye-witness authority as narrator of the events of that day, claiming his pride in his involvement with this new policy of indirect action, and turned out also to be the American missionary Chris Dove, director of the evangelical radio stations in South Lebanon, who gave information to Israeli intelligence in preparation for the 1982 invasion, the same person who appeared in the background of a photograph of President Betancourt receiving the members of the Kissinger Commission in La Paz, curiously at the same time that the Jackal was reported to have returned to Colombia, and apparently was the same Dove who in June, 1983, three months before the invasion of Grenada was appointed to the National Security Council as advisor on Caribbean affairs, having been a missionary in the islands.

His maps had woven all the disparate islands of information into a sure chart of recent history, the accuracy of which he had no doubt. He could pick up any newspaper of the past ten years and fit every item into his maps, confirming and reaffirming the veracity of both the event and the maps. And yet, the maps did not tell him why,

Christopher's question, Americans thought it was necessary to apply so calculatingly their efforts at controlling Latin America. Captured weapons in El Salvador showed very little Russian or East European involvement that could not be accounted for by the fact that the Somozas had imported large amounts of small arms from Eastern Europe during their reign. Cuban involvement was exclusively non-military, said government observers. Yet, the American press was full of general anti- communist hysteria, general because it was not even clearly about Communism or Communists. Think of what will happen if they start importing Latin American revolution to this country when there are 15 to 20 million Hispanics here now, said Senator Walla.

And what are US interests in Central America, anyway? It is not a very lucrative market, the people are so poor. It is not a rich source of raw products unless we invent a fruitmobile to replace the gasguzzler. We must simply not like them, and this seemed true, for as he pushed his research further into the past, he found that all the present patterns were old patterns redrawn, perhaps patterns ingrained in the American character as Christopher claimed. His maps became repetitive. All explanations of US actions against Nicaragua or Contadora were but excuses to continue an age old game. The US had invaded Latin American countries forty times, about once every five years, the first time, the taking of Florida, being justified in the negotiations for the Treaty of Paris even before the US was us.

This was a US history he did not know, a memory he could not recall, since some invasions had happened in his lifetime but he could not even say how many, five, six, Guatemala, the Dominican Republic, Grenada, Cuba, he could not say, totally remote, totally inconsequential to US living, and yet, he assumed, it was all being done for the sake of that living. But Latin American historians all knew the US Consular dispatches from South America formulating the anti-Bolivar policy of supporting local landed interests so that the US would not have to compete against a large, powerful neighbor, counseling us to refuse Bolivar refuge while publicly supporting this George Washington of SA, knew that Monroe's doctrine was hands

off for others and hands on for us, long before Roosevelt's aggres-
sions, knew the Americans who died at the Alamo had all been part
of a gigantic con game to grab Mexican land, all having sworn that
they were persecuted Irish Catholics seeking asylum to feed off
Mexican generosity, knew that the US marines occupied Nicaragua
for twenty years and only left when they had installed the Somoza
dictatorship as payment for the assassination of Sandino, knew that
all the southwestern states were ceded to us by a man the US marines
appointed to represent the Mexicans.

Every detail of these tales of infamy he learned seemed distasteful,
banal, and yet sinister, the reference in an American text to the US
engineered Panamanian revolution as bloodless except for the
incidental loss of a Chinaman and a dog, not different from the
humiliating scenes played out every Saturday afternoon in the pink,
hillside mansion surrounded by orange, yellow, and deep red bou-
gainvillea and tall palm trees above Cuernavaca where the Mexican
Minister of Finance, having driven up from Mexico City for his
lesson, would be given tea by the future Mrs. Lucky Lindy while her
father Mr. Morrow, the same Morrow for whom his college dorm was
named, Mr. Morrow, Cal's man in Mexico, in white flannels and high
buttoned blue blazer, cajoled, reproached, hindered, enervated,
stifled, dictated, bent, restrained, inhibited until Mexico's financial
activities for the week were planned satisfactorily.

Anglos did not like Hispanics, had not liked them for as long as
they had been burning Guy Fawkes, did not like them by policy,
Queen Elizabeth's, one formulated for her by Hakluyt, a great
geographer whose work he had never before seen as sinister, and by
Raleigh, one of England's great poets but now to him a senseless,
madly ambitious killer, a policy he could probably date precisely in
the year 1584 if he had access to a good Renaissance library, early in
the year when there must have been a meeting or some exchange of
letters between the nationalistic geographer and the insanely anti-
Catholic adventurer, a policy to infringe on the Pope's and therefore
the Spanish claims in the New World by propagandizing Catholic
cruelty among the natives, by a kind of political evangelicalism not

unlike, come to think of it, the American use of anti-communism, a policy carried out by Oxenham and Drake a decade before it was policy when they made stepping stones for the future British Empire by recruiting and organizing native tribes as freedom fighters all around the Caribbean, which is why the Miskit Indians in Eastern Nicaragua have English names and have always fought the Western Nicaraguan Spanish speakers and why an educated and well read CIA functionary named Dove suggested using the Miskits as a foundation for the mercenary contra army against the Sandinistas, a four hundred year old policy of militant evangelicism still functional, still stirring the anglo imagination though every facet of the reality it acted on was changed.

It was just as unfathomable as any other topography in his maps. Did these forms his maps documented have a life of their own? He did not like to think of himself as a fool of these large forms, and yet an Elizabethan geographer's idea had surely grown into actions in a world far beyond the life of the mind that invented it, and its growth and expansion were certainly through the agency of human action, and could these humans who performed the work of the forms be said to be individuals acting on their own volitions? Perhaps, it was worse, for he could only hypothesize that Hakluyt thought up the forms of the English stereotyping of the Spanish and that once invented the forms, like wayward children, outgrew their father and the governance of all humans, perhaps Hakluyt was himself a pawn for the emergence of these ideas, perhaps humans had very little to do with their actions at all, Hakluyt and Raleigh no different from Walter Zuleta or Christopher or himself, so that the only import of his maps was that Americans, too, simply act out their roles in a larger historical game. It was depressing.

Looking up from his work desk in one wing of the Lecumberri Archives at the lightness of the huge space embraced by the building's central dome, it seemed also ridiculous. Lecumberri was a monument to human rationality, and so to individualism, the human capacity to choose, to each person's will to determine his own fate, to the human spirit's triumph over nature, to the human world order. It was built to Jeremy Bentham's specifications for the panopticon inspection house, an idea of a new principle of construction applicable to any sort of establishment in which persons of any description are to be kept under inspection, and in particular to penitentiary houses, prisons, houses of industry, work houses, poor houses, manufactories, mad houses, lazarettos, hospitals, and schools, so we know where factory workers and students and sick people belong, a central dome, modeled on the Renaissance church, complete with its eye of God, and eight two-storied wings extending out like rays of sunlight enlightening the inmates kept in their individual cells along the wings and observed from one central tower under the dome's eye, the form, not unlike his maps, transforming the image of God's sight into reason's concern for human vigilance.

But, he remembered, on his first visit to this prison turned archives the year before, he had noticed that the dominating rationality of form reduced all individuality to some kind of equivalency. Going from wing to wing following a display of ancient maps, he had become lost and was baffled that the same maps were exhibited twice. The building was smaller than he had thought from the dome's impression of vastness and power: the circle had no direction, all sides were identical, as were all the cells each with one large window and one narrow door. This loss of direction and individuality gave the panopticon its peculiar feeling of well-being, airiness, light, and comfort, for the panopticon provided the serenity of invisibility, of an invisible participation and unity in space itself. To a certain extent, the individual was reformed into a community, or the loss of self was ameliorated by the gaining of community, though this community was not human society, being rather a kind of co-unity with space, with space and light and air, that is with sight, with the clear seeing of pure rationality. He felt strongly in this building that individual aberrations were better left behind to enter this great sun of reason. Like mathematics, the panopticon was a closed system, nowhere allowing the pessimistic notion that rationalism was itself a human aberration and that this magnificent architecture of prison reform, a physical emanation of the exuberance of Newtonian optics, was bound to fail, for this light hid the dread, terror, and pain of thousands of stories, Lecumberri having been a prison for political prisoners, those that would not or could not be made to disappear like Christopher, the national institute of political science, Paz called it, the last atrocity taking place on New Year's Day only six years before when 115 political prisoners, mostly arrested in the student disturbances of 1968, occupied the M, N, and C wings. Eighty-seven of them had begun a hunger strike 24 days before, 65 still being on lime and sugar. At night the prison's under-director unlocked the passageways and incited the common prisoners of F wing to attack the politicos. Armed with bottles, metal tubes, knives, razors, the common prisoners spent two hours beating the 68 political prisoners in C wing. The attack on M wing lasted only forty-five minutes. N wing became a place of refuge, but it too was finally ravaged. Every bit of personal belongings was systematically destroyed, mattresses, bedding, paper, books, manuscripts, limes, sugar, everything. How fitting that some Latin's admiration of cool English reason should cause Bentham's attempt to create a substitute for England's lost colonies, no place to transport to, to be built on this colonial side of the sea, since the freedoms that utilitarian rationality promised turned out to be as illusory in this building as in the country it created to the north, and fitting too that his maps should have led him back to this building, since they too denied the individual any freedom, submitting him to the similar forms of history.

7

On the way to the Embassy, he still did not understand how they had managed to garble Carol's message home after the earthquake and report him dead to his sister, who was afraid to tell his mother. He walked towards the Reforma behind an American mother and her college-age daughter, marvelling at the revival of bermuda shorts and wrap-around skirts after thirty years, print blouses with little round collars and pink Adidas, the mother with a dark blue cardigan sagaciously draped over her shoulders. He walked just behind them watching the lines on the back of the daughter's bare legs, when hearing the mother say, isn't that girl just lovely, he looked up to see an Indian girl about ten years old, grinning and skipping towards them. Her hair was tangled and matted, she had on a dirty green and white dress, slightly behind her and to one side were her brothers and sisters. Two older Indian women from the south, Guatemala or Chiapas, followed, very tiny, heavy bare feet pattering on the pavement, their black wrap skirts loose under their shawls. Very suddenly, one of them quickened her steps and reached the Americans before her daughter, who stopped her dancing. She held out her hand, cupped for alms, and just as quickly, the American mother stopped talking and looked away, brushing past the Indians. Her move was so dexterous he lost momentarily the sense of malice in it, seeing the wonderful pulling into oneself like a sudden recognition of purpose, so elegant and sure she must have been born with it.

If Indians were not quite invisible for Americans, as Christopher argued in one of his letters, they were certainly something like parts of the landscape, the most dangerous of the wild beasts of this continent, he remembered the clichés about the Indians' invisibility in the French and Indian War, the way they blended in with the wilderness, their silent travels through the virgin forests of the East, their bark eating ways in northern New York state, barbarians. Christopher said that the European settlers were escapees from culture, that they brought with them not the idea of going to another culture, like an Englishman going to France or even to China, where there were local laws to obey and customs to accommodate themselves to: going to America would not remind any settler of the old adage, when in Rome, do as the Romans. Coming to the virgin land meant coming to a land without people, and the idea of freedom that this escape inspired could only be actualized by making the land seem virginal, by eradicating the Indian, so this woman, who found Indians interesting, fascinating, and beautiful, did not express her feelings of sanctity or superiority in her elegant gesture, but her feelings of freedom, the right to pursue her own and her daughter's happiness, a European dream come true, fabricated true here in the new Europe.

If Lecumberri was the dream of rationalism, the Embassy was its reality, for underneath its functional modern, commercialized Bauhaus forms, the Embassy was a tenth-century fortress, the land filled in and built up, so that the building, six stories, square, repeated motifs of slab marble, sat on top a small hill, the approaching slopes all left open, so that the attacking forces would find no shelter from the projectiles aimed at them from the tower, mainly from the projecting balcony with two-foot thick balustrades all around the building and dominating all approaches, paranoia having been transformed into contingencies and these possibilities all translated into endless construction details. He found on closer inspection that there were no functional parts of the Embassy on the ground floor, it being only open space, as if the building were on stilts. His only ways into the tower were by elevators, which could be shut off by a master switch, and by a very narrow, doubled-back staircase that could easily be sealed or defended by one or two people, and in any case the second floor housed only the Agricultural Department and the IRS. The building had a central, open air garden, in cloister-garth style, which was commanded by interior balconies all around the second floor, so all the open space under the building was under lines of fire from this interior balcony. When he and Rihan with her Why-are-Americans-so-bad banner demonstrated against the American invasion of Grenada, the balconies were filled with marines in battle dress, their olive green camouflage standing out against the building's cream colored marble and concrete surfaces.

The palisade was made of 1 x 4 pickets of steel ten feet tall, a bit of Americana iconography, though unlike Tom's fence, the pickets were not mounted flat but edgewise, making a 4-inch thick steel wall, and were painted battleship grey. On two sides, where the hillock-platform reached almost out to the fence, the fence was backed by a five-foot high stone wall.

The building would seem to be well protected, from mobs as well as from small arms attacks, even from truck bombings, since you couldn't drive a truck over a five-foot stone wall onto the platform or penetrate a 4-inch steel fence and go up fifty feet of stairs under fire to reach the building from the front, but the previous month the Embassy usurped the sidewalk around the building and started adding three-foot thick cement blocks pretending to be twenty-foot-long flower boxes all around the fence on the curb. He had to walk in the street to get to the main gate. At the street crossings, the flower box design was abandoned in favor of cement filled steel posts.

Getting into the Embassy was not easy: at the palisade gate he had to present an ID with a photo, Carol had warned him to take his passport, under the building he had to explain that he wanted to find information about an American named Christopher Ng from the Embassy's registry of Americans in Mexico, who was Christopher Ng, did he work at the Embassy, was he related, which department did he want to go to, wait, I just want to register my address with the Embassy, see I'm an American, Office 345, you take this time indicated pass, go only to Room 345, do not pass Go, get the pass punched into the time clock there and return here. At the third check point, the marine took his penknife away. At the Office for Citizen Services, the man would not give him any information: we don't keep files that long, we are not allowed to divulge personal information that may be detrimental to the individual, you can understand our side of this, can't you, you wouldn't want us to give out information about you, we don't meddle with the internal affairs of Mexico, the individual must have been up to no good if he was deported or imprisoned, no wonder they took away his penknife, his five minutes were up, punch in the pass and leave.

On the way home he wanted to stop at the American Library, which had been temporarily moved to the top floor of a new office building near the Embassy after the earthquake cracked the cultural center in two, wanted to check the Directory of American Scholars in case Christopher returned to the US and became a professor somewhere. He was, after all, an intellectual and that was what intellectuals did in the US, but remembering the etiquette on all the books in the library, Dear Patron, This book has been carefully checked before lending it to you, therefore, we beg you to return it in the same condition, this book will be checked upon its return, if it is damaged or mutilated you will be accountable for its condition and replacement, plus a checklist with columns for the name of the checker, the pages checked, and the date, and resenting the identity check and search he had to go through to enter the library, he went to the French Library to relax in its leather comfort and read the journals.

Perhaps, he shouldn't be here in Mexico at all. He had come to work out his ideas on two-dimensional representations of visual reality. Instead, he was now conducting a private America watch. Like the China experts, sometimes reporters and sometimes intelligence agents, who hung around Hong Kong in the sixties on a China watch, he would be the first Chinese, maybe the second, to pursue an offshore America watch. But perhaps he should be in China, lecturing the students about the dangers of gringo culture. The Chinese were so gay about technology. They wanted to be just like the West, rational, progressive, and technological. They had forgotten the anonymous Chinese engineering student in his icy garret in Berlin warming his fingers and softening the stiffening brush over the small candle-flame in frequent pauses of working on China's *Defense* against the West. They didn't know that technology was capitalism was imperial domination and spiritual decline. He knew something about these things, all the technologies that went into modern mapmaking came out of mercantile expansion and the centralization of money, and they all declined rather than progressed. Take photography, for example. The most potent, the most beautiful photographic process, the photograph that still was the most essentially photographic, was the daguerreotype, its slightly pink and gold tints glowing out of the polished silver plate, and a human face hovering in that glow, like hanging smoke, the face shorn of temporal expression and so, revealing in this totally relaxed state the meditative, inner structure of the person, the first photographic process developed by Niepce in his Burgundian hillside town over a hundred fifty years ago. Every technological advancement in processing and in equipment has cheated us of the invented magic, because each advancement has been to make money and not images, until now we look dully at dull pictures, and it doesn't even matter that we have to see the world always in the optical strictures of lenses, he would say.

He could give them many examples, any invention, cars, light bulbs, batteries, cigarette lighters, watches, airplanes. They always had the same general story. The culprit was not always marketing tactics. The economics of replacement, for example, dominated technological advances in thousands of products, cars, tape-recorders, washing machines, typewriters, hot plates, toasters, stoves, refrigerators, electronic equipment, drills, electric saws, digital watches, thermostats, jitney trucks, alternators, sewing machines, vacuum cleaners, blenders, mixers, waffle irons, light switches, sockets, doorbells, steam irons: the stuff of American life, distinguishing it from Chinese life, is constantly advanced to make reparation impossible, because by transforming individual repairmen in small and middle-sized communities all over the country into factory workmen in large industrial cities, large companies can control more of the economy and more of the people, and so make more money as well as gain the option to transport the factories to China for cheap assemblage to make more money.

But when it came down to it, he was not in China. They would consider him bizarre, at best, speaking against the grain in broken, archaic Chinese like some unidentifiable foreigner, maybe like a Japanese who had learned his Chinese during the war, a bespectacled young intellectual drafted for administrative duties in the occupying army, a barbarian, a barbarian just as it turned out he was in America. He used to mention in his ancient geography course that the Greeks called foreigners babas because they spoke nonsense, thinking it a curious etymology describing the Greek mind, but Christopher had taught him that he, in fact, was the babaing black sheep, exempt not only from the sacrificial fires but from law altogether, without identity, and as invisible as the Indians were to the English, we stealthy, quietly bleating babas. Thinking of himself as Chinese, however, did not open a redolent world of heightened recognition, fragrances of ancient wisdom, the dry, dusty scent of a sandalwood box opened after a long interval, but instead, he felt the sham of his American habits, like stolen garments that fit too well. Europeans could become Americans, sometimes made better Americans than Europeans, but Asians, Africans, American Indians, Polynesians, Arabs, aborigines of the rest of the world could only pretend at it. Yet, he was as American as Christopher, so that if his former colleagues in America thought him a crazy man, in China they would think so too, a foreign ghost. He was here, instead, in Mexico, watching Americans and speaking broken Spanish, wondering how it all began. Columbus, of course, was sure this was China, the beginning of the east.

8

He could see Beto, head and shoulders above the crowd, in front of Doña Rosa's house. He stood on tiptoe and waved, shouting hey Beto, but Beto was looking in through the open doorway. Some of the women on the sidewalk turned to look at him, country women, heavy, short, shading their heads from the hot May sun with woolen shawls, mostly barefooted women, he imagined their flat feet against the pavement, drawing warmth out of the earth, and some men, too, wearing straw cowboy hats mass manufactured in Korea. He did not know what they were doing. They seemed not to be paying much attention to whatever was going on inside, but they stood about waiting and talking, nothing happened, as if we hadn't been there, nobody paid any attention, he could only make out bits and pieces of the talk in a quick, raspy accent he did not recognize, lucky not to get hurt, escape, didn't get hit, thanks to God. He squeezed through the crowd towards Beto, not even sure that his little murmured excuses were being understood. Near the door, leaning against the wall, were some placards and rolled up banners, Frente Nacional contra La Repressión.

Inside it looked dark and cool and quiet. On one of the sofas an Indian woman, her black hair braided with green and red yarn and tied up over her head, was talking with Doña Rosa. Except for a small group around the sofa, the rest of the women in the crowded room were just talking and waiting, not paying much attention to them, but the room was small, and he could hear the conversation quite clearly, in the morning, Sra. Rosario said, there's no need for us to stay more days here, no one's paying us any attention, but on the contrary, some people arrived who pulled on us, ripped our shawls and tore them to pieces, Na China Henestrosa, Beto told him, that night we were careful, there were some fellows from the White Brigade, they stood guard over us. Then a father let us into the church, he was a good Christian, one of the fathers said for us to stay, the other said that we had to leave, let them come in but they go out by five tomorrow, then, there were words between the fathers, one of them said, why are you throwing them out, so, you're against them, too, and with that argument they let us in, but the night was almost over, and that's where we stayed the rest of the days.

Her son had disappeared four years ago in Juchitan, a town in southern Oaxaca, kidnapped in broad daylight by men in army uniforms driving an orange VW van, no arrest record, no court records. The others all had similar stories. They had walked to the capital from all parts of Mexico to carry on a hunger strike at the cathedral and wait for a message from the president. I think we were there ten days, because the Señora, Rosario, said, every one of us has left our homes, but the government pays no attention to us, that whole day we were there and nothing, we were, we kept up the hunger strike in that place, I think it's called Santa Veracruz where we were with Sra. Rosario, we were also at San Hipolito, I think we were in San Hipolito eight days, a little less. Everywhere they didn't pay any attention to us, even though they promised everything, they didn't do anything, I was telling you about them, even though we went there, we dared to see if they would give us a good answer, but nothing, they didn't even give us hope. Still, we went there, to where Aliseo Ruiz was, we were there in the governor's palace where he was sitting, I went in, I talked with him. I told him, Señor, my son, Polin came in, Candida came in, well, Señora, he said, I don't know. I said to him, I know you, you were a teacher at a military school, a niece of mine used to be his student, she gives classes over there in the hospital, he said, where was that, in Tapachula, I told him, that's why when I learned your name, I said I would come in person, but since there were many people waiting, they didn't let us talk too long.

Hurry, hurry, hurry, because it was quitting time and he was getting ready to leave, but Polin made him sit down, his secretary was leaving, saying, now we're going, but there were lots of people, so we couldn't talk to him, until we gave him the letter that the Bishop of Tehuantepec gave us. He looked at it and then was giving it to, no, no, we told him, don't pass it on to, we brought it for you, for you to read yourself. So everybody, nobody, they didn't listen to anything.

Still, I wrote a letter to this one, the new governor, I sent him a letter, before he came into office, in which I said, maybe doing something for me and my son, I don't know him, but in my heart I feel he's a good person, but all the time when he wasn't yet in office, I thought when he comes to power, then I'll get it, sometimes, I wonder if they had given it to him or thrown it away, that's what I think, they're 100% enemies in there, because if he had gotten it, I think he would have answered me, I'm sure they didn't give it to him, even if it was there, it would happen that when they saw it they wouldn't tell him.

So, then, I was depressed, desperate, but I didn't stay that way, I always got out, I said to myself, why, I'm not going to stay put, it's o.k. to go, to go wherever they go, as long as someone doesn't drag me off, I'll go see, go listen to see that they don't fool me, I'll go see if someone mentions my son's name, always I'm going. And, now? I can't go anymore. Around Juchitan, nearby, maybe, I'll go to Chicapa, but to Mexico City, I can't go again.

When he left, Beto was still by the door listening, leaning against the wall, all his weight braced on one foot, looking very north American. Where had he learned that slouching, swaggering body movement so different from the tight, crisp, elegant bearing of the Indians around him? They would have to come back another day to get Doña Rosa's approval of the final form of the article. He went to El Encuentro to see Sr. Muñoz, but sitting in the dark across the small table from Sr. Muñoz, he had nothing to say to him. He had run out of questions about Christopher, and he did not know how to say what he thought of the manuscript. Sr. Muñoz's son had walked ten waterless days across the Chihuahua desert to get to the US, surviving a rattlesnake bite that, throbbing, puffed out his right hand like a melon, pursued by a border patrol helicopter that tried again and again to crush him with its skids, dislocating a shoulder before he was able to roll into a rocky gully for protection, spitting out the dry grit that filled his mouth, and two years later he took his wife and two small children on his back across the river. He was now installed in a camper-shell in some small New Mexican village breaking his already stooping body doing whatever labor too hard or too low paying for the gringos, looking forward to the children growing up American. He could not explain to this dark man wrapped still in the tragedy of the conquest what it was like to grow up in an always transparent present, immersed from childhood in stories where tornadoes and earthquakes turned out to be entrances into magical, fine worlds of fairness and justice, could not say, imagine the astonishment of a young Chinese-American reading in the all-night study room in the basement of his college library that nineteenth-century philosophical question, if you can attain all you want in life by simply wishing the death of a small yellow man on the other side of the earth, would you do it, did not want to say that Christopher was right to give up health, money, safety, comfort, education, whatever, his father's grocery business in Costa Mesa, California, a grant to do graduate studies in social anthropology, his small landscaping business in Rock Island, Illinois, in order to understand his own tragedy, that of a small yellow man, nor would he be able to explain why Christopher was wrong to think that the source of American culture could be found by mining his own character, habits, and beliefs.

The problem was historical, though personal, too, for his maps taught him to believe in a single and unique aspect to American history, and when he read of the American Secretary of State pounding the table in anger, the vertical stripes of his dark, double-breasted suit with too wide lapels bouncing up and down, so much like a bald-headed Los Angeles used car salesman, bouncing up and down in nasty fury at the Yugoslavian minister for suggesting that international terrorism could be eliminated by eliminating the imperialistic causes, or when he read today that the US immigration department had initiated deportation proceedings against an American professor, just bizarre, who had written that in Vietnam American imperialism had suffered its major defeat, then he was certain that history, at least American history, had to be a single, monolithic structure which, reaching back through time, explained the congruency of all the small individual outrages of American society. America was too uniform, too cohesive to be anything else than the slow accrual of a single historical process, on the basis of which every facet of American life, of his life as well as of Christopher's life, could be explained.

Christopher was wrong, he could not say this to the quiet, waiting man across the table, to ask why Americans were so bad, or rather, he should have asked the question in a more slanting way, as he did, what concatenation of circumstances and beliefs and methods produced a history which caused him, a person born in China over fifty years ago, able to trace his ancestry through eighteen generations of poets and painters, to be an American, speaking, writing and thinking American in an American world. Christopher was so concerned with his own identity and was so American, that he always pursued his answers directly, so he did not see that the problem was not why he was American but why he was not Chinese.

So he told Sr. Muñoz that he had learned a great deal from Christopher and was grateful, which was true, learned that ideas became real in the living of them, all other ideas, whether fresh as fragrant guayabas or canned in sweet syrup by Delmonte, were delected only in academies, kept like Indians on reservations from polluting the culture at large with debate and thought, and so learned, too, that he had become totally unfit for academic service in America, because the academy had become a teaching tradition rather than a thinking tradition, part of the same history he was tracing, requiring objectivity, non-commitment, professionalism, open-mindedness, practicality and efficiency, so that there was no room for single-minded fanatics, madmen like himself, Newton in his apocalyptic last volume of Biblical studies, Boehme, doggedly sewing together the pieces of a spiritual alchemy, Lull, the divine peacemaker, spinning the enlargening circles of his universal engine that was to demonstrate to infidels the cogged wheels of this God's creation, Marx myopically pursuing the logic of a single sentiment, willing to set aside five years worth of work to spend ten years filling in a gap in his knowledge that had suddenly come to light, no room for such universal minds as Coleridge, the greatest thinker in the English language, how, he thought, the tenure and promotion committees would dig their teeth into Coleridge's plagiarisms, the very sign of a lived idea, the always incomplete projects, his inability to concentrate on some worthwhile topic without hopping about and changing fields, for how could a man spread himself into so many areas without being terribly thin in them all.

Before going home he told Sr. Muñoz that sometimes disappeared people reappear, like Walter Zuleta, he said, telling one of the Zuleta stories, there's always a chance, but he had decided to go to Spain to pursue his suspicion that America had always been the same, that at the moment of discovery America had been formed, entire, complete, and for all future time, and to try tracing its original form in such a way that it would show the moment by moment formation of a future which included his and Walter's and Christopher's stories as well as those of Sr. Muñoz and his son and grandchildren. He would take intellectual activity, speculative history, out of the academy back onto the streets, where Christopher's manuscript assured him that there was a home for him. It would be healthy generally, even if his private madness was not, because in America the academy had absorbed so much of American intellectual activity, the poets, the painters, the printers, as well as the scientists and thinkers, cultural observers and writers, absorbed it all out of the culture into a closed panopticon. Today he had read the Mexican president's eulogy for Demetrio Vallejo, a left wing organizer, leader of the once powerful railroad workers' union, founder of socialist political parties, a man who spent eleven years in Lecumberri, and he tried to imagine America as an open society in which the president eulogized a jailbird, eleven years in prison and elected to legislature, unthinkable in America, so that most of what is lived as life in the rest of the world is as yet unthought in America.

At home he wrote his department chairman asking for a second year's leave of absence, keeping options open, they called it, and he wrote the university housing office asking them to rent his house to a visiting professor or sabbatical replacement. He told Carol that it would be enough if they did not live like Americans. He remembered a conscientious liberal telling him before he came to Mexico that it would be immoral to earn money at the American rate and spend it at the Mexican rate since it amounted to paying cheap wages while earning high wages. What hogwash, he suddenly burst out, surprising Carol, to imply that if one stayed in the US there would be equity. That's how the American economy is sustained, buy cheap abroad and sell dear at home. That very person drives a Japanese car, rides on Guatemalan tires, watches a Taiwan television set, heats his house with Mexican oil, all paid for at rates far below the American minimum wage, a dollar a day for the rubber plantation worker, who, in addition, is not allowed to live with his family off the compound. On the contrary, everything they spent in Mexico helped equalize the differences between the two economies, but it was still preferable, he had learned from Christopher, not to live like Americans.

PART TWO
SEVILLE

...fué por fuerza correr adonde el viento quiso.
                                    —*Columbus*

1

It had to have begun with Columbus, that enigmatic and stubborn bookseller whose lyrical memories of an Andalusian spring were awakened by the splendorous green vegetation of a world he suddenly came upon. It might have begun with Columbus' double log, that devious man recording in his public log a far shorter distance traveled every day than the actual distance he recorded in his private diary so his fearful companions would not know how far they had come from terra firma. But where had he learned to act like a Machiavellian prince, this self-taught wool gatherer pretending to be first a book man, then a navigator, then an admiral, then a prince, and finally a saint, and how had he been able to create in the midst of all these public masks and rhetorical poses a lyrical, private self? Somewhere here, in the forming of the world's first self-made man, in the creation of a functional schizophrenia, in desire, in deception, in power, in adventure, must lie the beginning of the modern world, which is, after all, America's world, and so he pored over Columbus' letters and journals, looking for some clue to the beginning, some sign, some unexpected disturbance erupting onto the surface of events as signification that might explain how it had come about that a Chinese-American should disappear from the slums of Mexico City, or a Salvadoran mestizo with an English name should be tortured by an American and a Chinese soldier in San Salvador, or why a Chinese Mandarin would be a scholar of European maps and be in Seville looking for the origins of American imperialism.

His differences with America were not a matter of political

opinion, not an alienation caused by his obsession with historical topography, not a deviation from his past: they were a return, for he felt prior to America, and being prior, as the world was prior, to America, he felt that he did not deviate from America, but America was the deviation in him. He had a line already set for him by history, long before America, or rather, he and the rest of the non-European world were living out the history of that first world event wherein the world became the home of various diverse and significant cultures, and the coming of America had intruded itself into that line, bent it, twisted it, absorbed him, and the world, into another history, a second world history. There were, after all, only two significant world events in history, one being the humanization of the world, the gradual migrations over hundreds of thousands of years of the various types of humanoids, gradually mingling into the human race populating the whole planet, and the other being what he was living through, what had occurred so rapidly in the past five hundred years, a sudden Europeanization of the world, a transformation of cultures into a single culture, a cultural Blitzkrieg whose major weapon was America. So there were many beginnings, for the explanation of America was also an explanation of the world to be, was also the beginning of the change in his destiny, and all the beginnings coincided in Columbus. Somewhere in the Colon papers would be a story, simple and empty like Walter's, something that filled out the interspaces of his maps, as if narrated by them, a story that contained his story and Walter's and Christopher's, history reduced to a simple story.

He looked hard for some, any, sign of that story, but in the end, there were too many stories to be meaningful. Colombo, Colon, Colonus, Columbus, Christofer or Cristovao, was as enigmatic as his name. He ended his life not knowing where he was, though it was unclear what he knew or did not know, what he believed or did not believe, whether he lied or dreamed, whether he manipulated others or was himself gullible, whether he was cunning, daring, capable, unscrupulous or was just an accident in history, whether he was possessed by an idea or merely invented an idea to excuse his failures.

When he first saw land and watched natives rimmed by the sun's halo paddling out to bring him presents, he decided to kidnap them. What for? Did he even then imagine a lucrative slave trade? He spent the next weeks looking for the mainland which he thought was the source of the gold trinkets his captives wore. How had he come to that conclusion? Through what converted Jew, adventurer, picaro, survivor speaking Hebrew, Caldean, or Arabic did he get this interpretation of the native babblings? Cristobal remained an enigma.

Outside, the blue neon hotel sign high above the Sevillan dusk was turned on for the night. The blue outline of a starfish was written across in red, Stella Mar. For six weeks when he first arrived in Sevilla he had read the sign as Stella Maria. Even when Carol asked him why the hotel used Stella instead of Estrella, since that's how you would have to say it in Spanish, the Spanish always has to say est instead of st, he had paid no attention and answered that it was just a foreign name used as a name, Stella by starlight, like Steinway didn't become Estainuei in Spanish: though Strasbourg became Estrasburgo, she said. And during the fall, when the letters started blacking out one after another, Carol would say, there goes the ess in Stella Mar, but he always registered the name as Stella Maria. One evening he suddenly saw that the blue outline, which he had always taken for a mod, free-form shape, like Hollywood swimming pools in the fifties, was in fact a five pointed star drawn with wobbly lines. Stella was, in fact, a star and not a name, una estrella. Right. So why was it Hotel Stella Mar instead of Hotel Estrella de Mar, Starfish Hotel?

Perhaps the Colombo problem was like that. Perhaps the second or third or tenth time he read Colombo, the beginning of it all would be as clear as a star. He returned to the archives of the Colombina Library. Everyone claimed him: the Catalonians said he was Catalan, the Jews, he was Jewish, the Portuguese, that Fernando Zarco sired him on a trip to Italy, the Gallicians said he was the son of a Gallician pirate, but he insisted he was Genoese and yet his nostalgia is stirred by the memory of an Andalusian spring. In his last Will and Testament, he referred mysteriously to the weight of guilt he bore towards Beatriz Enriquez, mother of his son Fernando, that dandyish, scholarly boy who was always something like a talisman for Colon, perhaps because he was the child of love, unlike his older half-brother Diego who was the child of duty, or perhaps because Colon mistakenly thought he was born the year he stumbled on America, but for what reason he felt guilt towards Beatriz we do not know and he would not say, adding only that it was illicit to discuss it in his Testament. His whole life was fabricated of delicate insinuations, gossamer hopes, intense desire, outright lies that were so bold they caught at one's fancy. The pitiful fourth voyage, which he ended bedridden and in debt, was narrated in his last letter to Isabella in the most sensitive, self-revelatory intimacy, and yet if it were to be believed, one would have to believe that at last he had discovered King Solomon's mines and that though he had almost been there, he could not, as in a dream, find his way back again.

His father, or was it his father before him, had been a master weaver in Genoa, he had said, but he had left home young to go to sea, an illiterate talker with a gift for learning and a stubborn belief in his own destiny: he had taught himself to read and write both the vernacular and Latin, had enough mathematics to navigate and draw charts, but ten years later, when he returned to Genoa to seek his roots, a trip never mentioned in any extant records, he could not find the weaving shop: the streets had changed, the building may have been there but only memories, oh, yes, a Colombo family, there in the next corner building, and not a trace of his cousins. And how was it that he could speak not a word of Italian though he could make out the Genoan patter in the streets, they looked at him as a foreigner with his bad Castilian mixed with Portuguese? He had taught himself to write the way he spoke, forcefully, with assurance, but in a mixture of Castilian and Portuguese and Latin. Perhaps he really was the son of a Gallician pirate who had taken the name Colon from the destitute young Genoese he met on the dusty road outside Seville and from whom he had also stolen a pair of leather boots.

He was so certain of his own fabrications that he not only believed them but made them come true, perhaps that is where America begins, in the strange alliance between failure and success, between

invention and discovery, between fable and history, between imagination and self-deception, that this man created out of his assurance.
He was sure before the second voyage that the large land mass west
of Espaniola had a continuous coastline and so had to be the south-
eastern coast of the Chinese province of Mangi, his mother's ances-
tral home, the furthest extent of the Great Khan's control, skirted by
Marco Polo two hundred years before, on his voyage home. He was
as certain of this as he was the first time he sighted the off-shore
islands on the first voyage. He could see the traces of the Pinto ahead
of him. For days they had seen signs of land, long seaweeds called
botelho and by others called asses' tails floating by, birds called belly
rippers high overhead, sticks and land grasses, a bramble of seaweed
with a crab astride, but that day as he watched the cresting fluorescent traces in the sea, he could smell the land in the air. In the
morning watch Pedro Gutierrez had reported that a green junco had
been seen. At noon, the longboat from the Niña had brought him a
carved staff the men of the Niña had fished out of the water, tall as
the height of a man's shoulder, of some reddish and tight wood that
weighed like iron. Rodrigo Sanchez, the King and Queen's man, said
the carved figure on it was a monkey, but it had a long pointed tail
like a dragon and its skin was like turtle shell. He held the monster
staff now as he felt the land rushing towards him, and he was already
in a state of relief and relaxation when he saw a flicker of light. Pedro
Gutierrez, climbing up to the poop, confirmed the light that could
barely be seen but moved up and down flickering like a candle.
Rodrigo Sanchez, the King and Queen's man, denied it, no, no mi
capitán, it's only the light of the Pinto, but he was certain, Rodrigo
be damned, so he announced that the first to sight land would earn
a bolt of the finest china silk, though everyone knew he hadn't any
silk, but it was the measure of his certainty, and indeed, at two in the
morning, Rodrigo de Triana sighted land, so there, Rodrigo Sanchez,
you may report that to the King and Queen, which he did, adding
that Rodrigo de Triana never received the bolt of silk because the
Admiral himself claimed the prize for having sighted the lights first,
even before he offered the incentive.

Again, there was nothing, nothing but Colon's insistence, an insistence that for all its errors of judgment, for all its mistaken calculations and for all its misinformation, turned out to be correct. The fact is, that if Columbus did not discover Solomon's mines, he did discover mines worth thousands of Solomon's mines, and how was this bizarre form of correctness to be correlated with that sense of familiarity Columbus and his men found in the new world, new, exotic, adventurous, yet recognized, perhaps like visiting one's dreams, so they found the native languages no problem at all. They asked questions and gave sermons, converted and baptized, proselytized, propagandized and assumed they were understood, hey, you understandee English, and they were. When they found gold trinkets, they asked for them, took them, and when looked at incredulously by the natives, they marvelled at the Indians' naïvete in giving whatever was asked for. Cristobal was genuinely touched by the natives' lack of self-assertion, so unlike him, and took upon himself the task of teaching them, but if he was touched he was also repelled, repelled by their naïvete, by their brutishness, by their naked as the day they were born way of inhabiting space, going in and out of the water with no consciousness of the difference between the elements, standing in the rain, water pouring from the mothers suckling their babies without even shielding their unprotected faces, standing there as if in sunshine, so that it was with some slight, perverse pleasure that he gave them rattles and glass beads, all of very little value, he proudly noted in his letter describing that first encounter the morning after Rodrigo had sighted land.

Of course, Christofer was a madman, too. He threatened everyone on his second voyage, with fines and with ghastly tortures, cut out their tongues, to make them all swear that Cuba was the mainland of China, but the problem, as always, was that his craziness had everything to do with his accomplishments. The lesson he learned from Cullumbus was that a man who thinks an island is a continent and the continent, an island, a man who says he is the messenger of God, claims to have found both the Earthly Paradise and King Solomon's mines, who insists that the earth is not round but round with a woman's breast on one side, the nipple being the Edenic garden of delight, he argued, could and did find gold, create a new world, and change the history of all mankind.

It was a purely Western phenomenon, he thought. Colon's story was not unlike the story of Western science, full of mistakes, it always worked. The gasoline engine was a mistake that had killed more that 2,500,000 people in the US alone, more than American dead in all its wars, comparable to the Holocaust, not to think of the money, the pollution, and the energy crisis with its attendant wars and sufferings, but the automobile was a success because it worked. Western technology, based on kinetics, that is, on force and movement, ultimately on the ideal of energy, spread like a disease all over the world, self-propelled, and threatened to annihilate the world, and yet it kept on bringing in the gold. Somehow the West could not be denied: success and power were its fate, but since success and power were its origin and its aim, the story is redundant.

An archer reported that he had seen men dressed in long, white robes. In the woods, cries of birds and animals were so loud and constant they were like a heavy silence that blended with the heat. The men resented being sent into the woods to hunt, and they made excuses to return to shore, where they felt the sea breeze creep through the joints of their armour and the sudden cooling on their streaming faces and necks, but the report of the men in white may not have been one of these cases. He questioned the archer at length, threatening to abandon him on the island if he lied, but all he could make out was a quick glimpse of something fleeing through the dense undergrowth, first standing upright and still and then crouching, crashing crouched through the branches and leaves, the birds and animals above joining their noise to the crackle and rush of the flight.

Carajo, who was he, this tall blonde man with an aquiline nose who stood in the stoney shade of the monastery gateway with his small son Diego begging for a piece of bread and some water from the doorkeeper, yet who had married into one of the oldest and most influential Lisboan families, and how, carajo, had he managed that,

he a vagabond, jack-of-all-trades, sometime sailor who had picked up
Hebrew, Caldean, and Arabic in his trips around the Mediterranean,
north past England, south into Africa to Guinea? He tried to imagine
him on the streets of Seville like Velasquez's water seller, peddling
yellowed and dirty pergamon bound books and scrolls of sea charts,
or dressed in new clothes, astride a donkey riding through the
burgeoning greenness of springtime Andalusia on his way to Granada,
to Court a second time, repeating into memory the passages of
Ptolemy and Saint Augustine, of Aeneas Sylvius and Seneca, of
Marinus of Tyre and Marco Polo, of Petrus de Ailliaco and Alfragan,
of Macrobius, reviewing the questions the Fray Talavera had asked
him years ago, the first time he presented his request to the Majesties,
the questions that pained him still now six years later, recalling with
a feeling of vengeance his recent talks with Pinzon who had told him
the story of the Queen of Sheba's voyage to Sypanso, which they
agreed must have been Cypango, the island empire off the east coast
of China, or he thought of him in dark, candle-lit conspiratorial
whisperings with his brothers, pouring over Petrus de Ailliaco's
world geography, recalculating Ailliaco's measurements and figures,
60 degrees, not 68 degrees, 60 degrees, it's shorter and closer even
than Ailliaco says, a few days westward, not much farther than twice
the length of the Mediterranean Sea, to the Levant and back, Ailliaco
was right about Ptolemy's error and besides he did not know about
Cipango, which Marco places 30 degrees East of Catai, or he imagined him in the sweet night Caribbean air, lying on his hands
masturbating, his son Fernando asleep beside him, pitching with the
ship, his eyes tight, shut, remembering the sliding warm sensation
going into Beatrice and feeling the welling up and tightening in his
center, now, or he tried to imagine him, hair already white by thirty,
said his son, peeping through the pinholes of his quadrant, balanc-
ing and compensating but never doubting or guessing when to yell,
ya, ya, take the reading ya. But he could not. Columbus remained
unimaginable without character, without soul, without even a name,
for when Colombo latinized his name he called himself a tiller of the
earth rather than a dove and so invented his Spanish name Colon

which made no sense unless his name never was Columbus or unless he mistakenly thought columns, colons, colonists, doves, and farmers were all the same thing, and so he remained without identity, inhuman though full of determination and argumentation, action, strategy, and tactics. He could not even be sure of the simple details of Colon's life. Was he tall and blond with an aquiline nose as every stock description pictured every prominent figure in the fifteenth century, like those identical, small woodcuts of a few houses, a town wall, and a church variously labelled Strasbourg, Urbino, Pavia, Sevilla, Nuremburg, Venetia, Bologna, Leyden, Tordesillas, Tarascon, or Geneva, he saw in Pierre d'Ailly's Imago Mundi, or like that bit of revealing and concealing anecdote mentioned both by his son Fernando and by De las Casas that Colon's strongest oath was by San Fernando, which is a commonplace in saints' lives, hire gretteste ooth was but by Seinte Loy?

2

When he came again to that passage at the end of Columbus' *Relation* of his third voyage in which he argues that the earth is a woman's pear-shaped breast with a tit on the top, he imagined how Columbus thought of sailing uphill, considering Colombo's argument that about 100 leagues west of the Canaries the climate suddenly grew milder, balmy breezes blowing gently towards the west, while his compass refused to hold steady, and that at night taking readings on the polar star, he saw it dip and rise crazily, how no one but a madman could think that going west he was getting closer to heaven and thus to warmer and more pleasant Elysian fields, but hardly had he taken up again his favorite theme of Columbus' insanity, when he realized his own foolishness, for he had been unable to relieve himself of his own twentieth-century certainty as to the shape of the earth, the shape he had shown Rihan in the photograph taken from the moon, for he had forgotten that Columbus' certainty was greater even than his own and that for him to understand the surprise of Columbus' discoveries he had not to think of an unknown part of the world becoming illuminated but to imagine a sudden, radical change in the shape of the world itself, to imagine, for example, the story of someone in the twentieth century: Bo, he called him, walking in the northwestern mountains of Montana, in a wilderness area he did not know, though he had hunted every year as a teenager in a section a hundred miles to the north, the pines and cedars fragrant in the dry summer air, walking and climbing a hill whose summit he seemed never to reach, stopping now and then to check the geological survey map he carried in the back pocket of his worn jeans, climbing further, strange, for he knew that he was west of the Divide and eventually would go down, but climbing steadily for days, for months, through winter blizzards of incredible force, going uphill, for years, until in old age he realized that no hill could be so tall, that climbing for a lifetime he had gone, by simple trigonometric calculation, not just a mile or two above sea level, but over 23,000 miles up and had long ago as a young man passed where Idaho should have been, and though the land was still somewhat familiar, the pines now grew amidst dense growths of orange trees and blowing bushes with giant yellow blossoms and blood-red leaves, broken here and there by large flooded plains that cut into the forests and where people grew a kind of slender grass from which a grain was harvested. This man Bo, he thought, walking his life away uphill, would surely think that the earth he had known as a boy had somehow grown an enormous cancerous boil on its side: no, bigger than that, he thought, more like the projection maps in his ninth grade geography book imaging the world on two overlapping circles grown bulbous, like the deformed hybrid tomatoes his father grew, and what would Bo think when one day, the sun still low and the morning mist still above the river, he drifted around a promontory in his small raft and came upon such an expanse of vessels in the water that it covered the whole width of the widening river almost three miles across, thousands, perhaps tens of thousands of boats, so many vancans, lanteaas, and barcasses filled with all kinds of foods, both of the sea and of land, pigs and tortoises, frogs, otters, adders, eels, snails, lizards, and red deer that were herded like sheep along the banks of the river, lamed in their front right legs to keep them from running away, dogs that were kept in large parks for breeding, dried orange peels with which in restaurants they boiled dog's flesh, to rid it of its rank and humid flavor and to make it more firm, all in such abundance that he could hardly imagine it, seeing sometimes two or three hundred boats together, full of the same produce, and all these vessels coming together to form a great town on the water, four or five miles long, made up of twenty thousand vessels besides the balons, guedees and manchuas, which were the smaller boats, infinite, all ordered by some complex, invisible government whose visible hands were some forty captains who kept the ranks orderly and thirty more to guard the merchants' safety under a chaem who had absolute power to judge civil and criminal cases, a town so vast that moving slowly downriver, changing and adapting its size and shape to the riverbank as if it were part of the river water itself, it yet maintained over two thousand streets, all very long and straight, formed of ships covered with silks and decorated with all colors of banners, flags, and streamers advertising their wares, and along these streets traveled quietly and peacefully the little manchuas hawking their merchandise, wu kuai, wu kuai chien i da, in a language he still had difficulty making out. At dusk, lanterns were lit and hoisted high on the masts, so that as night came the rocking, flickering shadows formed sharply in the brightness of the yellow light and anyone going in or out along the streets after retreat sounded, after the ropes were drawn across the streets, could be seen and reported the next morning by the street's appointed merchant guard to the chaem when his boat navigated all the streets clanging its sentinel bell, all the boats answering in a great, harsh din, and he wondered why such a large, brightly lit city would not be seen by passing airlines on the Chicago-Seattle run until he remembered that possibly through a deviation of the earth's magnetic field, this whole half of the globe had remained hidden from radar detection, satellite photographs, air space penetration, for so he had once decided, or perhaps, it was some more mysterious kind of plasmic field which could only be penetrated by the expenditure of life itself, a special kind of messianic energy, which he was certain was the only reason he had kept walking all these years.

The next day, awakening to the banging of the bells and paddling his raft into a section of town which he had not seen before, he saw a street of more than a hundred boats full of idols of gilded wood in the shape of feet, thighs, arms, heads, intestines, hearts, lungs, stomachs, and other parts of the body, which sick people bought for offerings in the various chapels framed on the great barcasses, one on every street, even in the poorest parts of the town, barcasses like ancient galleys, decked with silk and gold cloths, where priests received the offerings and laid out the sacrifices on incense reeking altars, and near these boats, with their piles of ex votos, were other ships covered with silk hangings, forming wide stages wherein comedies and other plays were presented to entertain the passing crowd, some stopping hypnotized by a story of a castaway sailor named Tobalito Ferrens, who built himself a great trading empire from nothing, lived almost five hundred years, and became an insatiable storyteller, while others busily passed by, not even noticing the clacking sticks the actors used to punctuate their declamations, jostling their canoes to get to the boats where they bought bills of exchange for heaven, without which their immortal souls would forever wander outside the eternal place of rest, or to get to those other boats filled with dead men's skulls, which people bought to put on the graves of their friends when they died so that when their friends mounted to heaven they would be accompanied and served by the souls of the people whose skulls were buried with them and, thus attended by such a large following, they would impress heaven's gatekeeper into letting them in, for clearly the poor shall have as difficult a time finding peace in afterlife as in life, or to get to the boats covered with cages of live birds singing to various stringed instruments while their owners strumming away exhorted the passers-by in song to free a captive bird so it could carry a message to god about the redeemer's good deed, and on all sides freed birds fluttered off, the buyers calling out their names to remind the birds of their messages. Next to these bird sellers Bo found the fish sellers whose boats were crowded by large earthenware jars filled with small darting shadows of fish below the wavering flashes of sunlight, and imitating the bird sellers, these were offering people a chance to send messages to the house of smoke below in the watery deep. On a side street he found boats piled high with animal horns being sold by priests who said that these were horns of animals sacrificed to gods on various occasions, sicknesses, broken arms and legs, earthquakes, when someone's house burned down, sudden losses on the futures exchange, and misfortunes, and that just as the earthly flesh of the animals were, after the ritual sacrifices, given to the poor to eat, so the horns could be burnt and sent to heaven as food for one's dead friends, so they could feast and invite their friends to feast and enjoy themselves in heaven. He saw also barcasses of bands and orchestras and choral groups that performed for hire. He saw black ships covered with mourning silks full of caskets, torches, great wax braziers, and women dressed in black who hired themselves out to weep and mourn for the dead. He saw pitaleuses like great floating zoos with serpents, huge adders, monstrous lizards, tigers, and snarling hyenas. He saw a great number of book sellers with books on the creation of the world, on geography, showing countries, oceans, islands, on laws and customs of unknown nations, on history, books of fables, poetry, plays, herbals, books full of diagrams and numerical calculation, some boats carrying books on only one subject, others carrying a great variety. He saw light, swift foists with their sails furled and all the men in them well armed, striking fierce poses, arms akimbo, one leg propped on the gunwale, while their leaders shouted that if anyone had been insulted or bullied these men were ready to avenge him, the terms being easily arranged to everyone's satisfaction. He saw in boats old women who served as midwives to help skillfully in birthing and in other boats nurses who would give suck to babies. He saw boats of old men and women whose business was to arrange marriages and engagements and also to comfort widows and widowers or children who had lost parents or parents who had lost children. He saw numberless small craft with young men and women looking for work of all kinds, servants, cooks, washing women, plasterers, carpenters, plumbers, ironworkers. He saw people in boats who told fortunes or found lost objects. He saw what no one else had seen before, no one except the hundreds of thousands of inhabitants of this far country, and what he thought, this Bo from Montana, could be no more bizarre than what Colombo imagined.

America was bizarre but also familiar: that was the difficulty of understanding the discovery and probably was the source of the European trauma over America, for comparing Columbus' accounts with Galeotto Perera's sixteenth-century description of the Chinese river scene he had imagined Bo seeing, he found that America conjured up problems of cosmology and ontology that the early European contacts with China did not threaten, for the discovery of America completed the world. Before Columbus the world had no particular definition, a terra incognita always allowed a spongy sense to existence, even if intellectually and abstractly the spherical shells of the Ptolemaic universe closed everything off, but the discovery fixed the world's limits, and thereafter, man lived in a different world, directly facing those limits, thereafter there was no thereafter, for America was the spatial equivalent of the Apocalypse, so Columbus seemed to have realized writing in a letter to the King that Saint Augustine and others had placed the end of the world in the seventieth century and that from the creation of the world and of Adam to the coming of Our Lord Jesus Christ was five thousand three hundred and forty-three years, and three hundred and ten and eight days, according to King Alonso, onto which we add one thousand and five hundred and one, imperfectly, making in all six thousand eight hundred forty-five, imperfectly, and therefore it only lacked one hundred fifty-five years to complete the seven thousand years at which time the world will end. And, indeed, the conquest and the result of that conquest had all the signs of revivalism and destruction that characterize the second coming, that is, a return, a turning back upon oneself that America was for the Western culture, a point of return, Columbus' paradise regained, atop his unknown mother's breast. Could the story that contained all other stories turn out to be Adam and Eve's?

Every morning upon rising, he drank sour milk from his blue Chinese cup, and every evening after dinner, he recited to Carol and Rihan the passage he had copied out of Hakluyt's *Voyages* by Galeotto, the Portuguese merchant shipwrecked and imprisoned in China, to the effect that the Chineans are the greatest eaters in the world, they do feed upon all things, specially on porke, which, the fatter it is, is unto them the less lothsome, and he hoped he would not get hepatitis as his sister had done and be unable to eat whatever he wanted.

3

Seville was Columbus' town, for overlaying the medieval Moorish citadel, its gold and cobalt blue tilework dazzling the Mediterranean sunlight, the cool spray of fountains and the dark, shaded green orange trees hung with oranges like small lanterns casting their calm delight against the harsh desert world, its fragrant gardens of pleasure, its loci amoeni, was the modern, commercial world Columbus invented. The wide thoroughfares cut through and cut up the narrow walking streets of the ancient quarters, and along these boulevards, whose names were a mnemonic of Columbus' voyages, like the names of the Galapagos Islands, were scattered the hundreds of local, state, national, and international banks that grew out of the daily hubbub of bartering and trading and profit-taking that took place on the Cathedral steps once Columbus returned from the first voyage. Every ship, every person, every thing that went to the Americas, or to any of Spain's overseas possessions, and every ship, every person, and every thing that returned came through Seville: the four hundred dozen poor quality German knives that Magellan took with him around the world, spreading world-wide the European principle of price adjustment, soft contact lenses are manufactured for fifty cents, bought by Bosch and Lomb for three dollars, sold to optometrists for fifty dollars, and retailed to the wearer for one hundred dollars, still the same piece of cheap plastic, Oviedo's cargo of barrel hoops that he used to make hatchets which could not hold an edge, so that in three months the Indians would have to buy new ones, which were only the old, bent ones straightened and resharpened and from which Oviedo made 8,500 castellanos, teaching us all the principle of built-in obsolescence, the large-headed mastiffs the conquistadores used for hunting Indians, the gold sun and the silver moon as big around as ox-cart wheels and carved with arcane Aztec figures that Moctezuma presented Cortez on the Vera Cruz coast through the emissary of Montalbor, an Aztec so resembling Cortez that the Spanish called him the other Cortez, brought to Seville to be melted down in the special foundry set up by the House, that corporate body which handled every bit of overseas affairs from the construction of public and private buildings to mapmaking to judiciary and episcopalian systems to prostitution, buying and selling human beings, lumber, pearls, peas, corn, cochineal beetles to destroy the two thousand year old kermes dye industry in Extremadura, the House which represented the first major corporate cartel in the world, a joint venture between government and private business, modeled on the contract signed between Columbus and his royal Majesties, and in whose empty, high-ceiling House next to the Cathedral he sat every morning scarf-wrapped, puzzling out the curlicue abbreviations of Columbus' and the royal scribes' handwriting, o th sd tnth day o mar, th adm rec 3 masks wth 19 pcs o gld lf, & 2 mirrors wth edges md o gld lf, & 2 cookng dshes mde o gld lf whch a bro o Cahonabo brght tht d, & mre o th ll o th sd mnth, one mask wth 10 lfs o gld whch he hd fr ransom, & mre o th sd dy people lft n hs rm 2 hammocks, & 2 lrg bndls & 11 rlls o cttn thrd, whch h hd fr ransom, & n th 4th o apr they lft i hs rm th following thngs whch were obtaind fr ransom, 25 pcs o naguas wd, 15 hammocks, 6 arrows, one wden machete, 9 Indn adzes, 1 woden trumpet, one feather drss, 6 pces of woven palm lfs, 14 parrots, 3 arrobas & 21 lbs of cotton thrd, poor Columbus.

The morning before Christmas day, he sat in front of his window groggy from the night's reading, eating his ritual Mongolian sour milk breakfast, staring past the tops of the giant eucalyptus and ceiba trees. Above the park hung the Hotel Stella Mar sign. He started suddenly. It didn't say Stella Mar. There was something else outlined against the blue starfish. He took the binoculars out of his drawer.

Stella Maris, Stella Maris, it read in yellow against the blue background. Good grief, the star Colon navigated by.

It was not competence, skill, knowledge, and expertise that brought Columbus to America but error, ignorance, lies, empty promises, and failure. His inability to cope with even the command of the expeditions, this dreamer whose sense of his own importance compensated for his openly despised inadequacies, a self-taught man among scholars, a commoner among nobility, a poor weaver among international traders, a perpetual foreigner, this incapacity to deal with the reality around him, was apparent on Christmas Eve during the first voyage when he ran the Holy Mary aground in calm, clear waters with only a mere boy at the helm and in his inability to keep Pinzon from sailing off by himself in search of gold, and again in the second voyage out, he could do nothing to prevent raiding parties pillaging and raping the Indians, so when he arrived at his settlement La Navidad and found all the men slaughtered as reprisals by the Indians for their raping the women, each Spaniard trying to keep a harem of five girls for his lust, he saw clearly the consequences of his inadequacies, there, stretched out on the very beach where the Santa Maria had been grounded two years before, the ten disfigured and bloated bodies, strange, he had paid so little attention to them while alive that he could not even now realize how unrecognizable they were, even Beatrice's cousin, and on their inland trek to S. Tomas, he could only stand back and watch the wreckage from the greed and lust which his dreams and desires had unleashed, no, more than that, fired and generated, which he had created as part of his scheming and calculations to realize his rightness, the fruit of his labors. My God, my God, he, a pious man, a peaceful man whose greatest oath was a mere exhalation, oh, but was he not just as evil, not having been content to sow the seeds of greed and lust, he had led them step by step here to this place, brought them from the first hint of gold to this massive desire, had seen the good-natured Indian friendliness as docility, their ignorance of iron weapons as weakness, had suggested their domination and usefulness as slaves, had traded their immortal souls as lucre and had he not been the first to reach out and touch the tan, brown breasts of an Indian girl under the guise of philosophic enquiry, she was no better than a whore to tempt him with her nakedness, had he not brought them here to rob and despise and rape and beat and kill these sons and daughters of Adam and Eve, as the caballero Pedro Margarit called them? He could not stop them, whip them, slit their noses, hang the rebellious louts: he could do nothing with these ungrateful and ignorant brutes who turned the mission of God into one catastrophe after another, and in the end he joined them, ignoring the Queen's specific command, himself ordering the taking of slaves, for how else could he fulfill the promise that he had made to the world to bring back riches beyond dreams, the gold now being clearly beyond him, the Indians no longer being as friendly or as docile and his own officers and friends and perhaps Bartholomew himself plotting behind his back, so he feared another inland expedition to the gold mines in the mountains, how else but to transport at least three hundred Indians for whom he could gain enough to pay for the ships, for in Seville alone he knew many eminent families that would pay well for docile and rare servants.

His years as a traveling banker's agent had taught him, perhaps, not only to distinguish his dress from that of the men of Mars, with their flowing dash and outdated legacy of a warring past, to merge his demean into the universality of the courtier, who could show by a word the force of his intellect, by a touch the certainty of his soul, learned not only to inspire confidence, care, knowledge, strength of character, but also learned value through continual exchanges with denaries, sterling, soles, florins, sequins, matapans of Venice, Islamic dirhems, cornados, escudos, marcs, maravedis, francs, reales, doblas, enriques, sceattus, solidus, hardis, from France, ambrosinos, ducats, ecus d'or, bracteates of the North he had once seen in England, augustrales, Rhenish imitations of florins, manuses, perperes, besantes from Istanbul, the noble Agnus Dei in gold, silver thalas from Malta, old marabotinos, and the new testones with the heads of Galeazzo Sforza of Milan or Giovanni Bentivoglio of Bologna or of Charles or from Turino of Philibert of Savoie, the whole mapamundi a banker laid out in front of him as he reduced it all to a single scale of value with his small, wire hand balance, for underneath the ephemeral forms and shapes of all money was a certain, plain, universal value, and he learned that this single and only value was what was important, the glitter of gold, made by God, into which all the earthly, man-made coins could be translated, so that money to gold was like the growlings and gruntings and lispings and trillings of the languages of men to the cleanly sure tongue of Adam as he named the things of creation in a language that was God's intellect itself. Superior to the merchant, who could only make money, buy low, sell high, converting goods into money, forever trapped in the circles of time and geography, the banker could make money from money and reach into the purely intellectual world of gold-shine, the world of essences into which he had sailed for the first time three years before and whose sure signs were the sweetness of the air and the heat which all men knew descends to earth from the pure region of fire, which is the heart of gold. Money, he knew, was only form, the princes of today stamping their effigies on it, but as the earthly powers changed in time and locale, the images changed, so their futile attempt to tie themselves to the permanent substance that held the forms, melted away as sighs, and the only use of money was as change and exchange, circulation endless, providing some with riches and others with poverty, changing hands, the rich fall, the poor rise, Fortuna's wheel turning, but the only real value was gold, the matter itself, which did not change, neither diminished in the world nor grew, until now. True increase could be gathered only by penetrating into the intellectual world of gold, an anagram for God, as he had explained to the Genoese merchants when he went to them in Seville, not as a merchant to bankers to borrow money against time, but as a banker to merchants, confident in his thoughts but made even more confident by his gestures, those courtier movements he had once watched so astonished, but which he had learned, startled at first that they worked, produced smiles and invitations, provoked a tone of response that ensured success, that now were second nature to him, facing the merchants, speaking with certainty in his mixture of Genoese, Portuguese, and Spanish, sure that they, too, found this lingua franca comfortable, advising as a banker that his venture was no mercantile undertaking but a direct reaching into value itself. It was an investment, for how could merchants, even with their two for three tactics, ever attain to true value if they existed only in a closed world, changing and exchanging money, wealth circulating, giving up value as well as receiving value to keep the wealth circulating. Can you imagine, he said, a ship of merchants with all the goods of life, passing goods and money amongst themselves, meanwhile using up the goods, why it is only a ship of fools. The only real step towards true value comes by opening the world, by expansion, by usurping new value, by bringing into the world value, so that the overall wealth increases, for which purpose bankers exist. Merchants exist for circulation, but bankers, for accumulation, which is what he had proposed with the word investment, dignifying and giving value to a simple exchange, an inversion, offering these simple men sunken into the worldly materiality of their daily lives a chance to rise to speculation, an alchemical philosophy of true conversion, for what was the exchange of goods for money compared to the transformation of debt into gold. No, in fact, he was the supreme banker: he was prepared to create, not transform, the nothingness of debt into the absolute value of gold, to produce value from faith.

It was a wholly new world he had opened up for them, a world without horizons, or with movable horizons always available for expansion paid for, created he had insisted, out of the nothingness of debt, a world of automobiles and video equipment, computers, plastic pens, cigarette lighters, washing machines and synthetic jackets, a complete and full world of things, matter, created out of the massive accumulation of debt, and debt was no simple nothingness, no dark hole of negative space, but a fully architectonic structure of debt instruments, bonds, certificates, bills, convertibles, long term, short term, high yield, low yield, tax free, junk, paper, terms, points, debt on debt, debt on debt on debt, discounted, coupons, OIDees, buying and selling debt on debt on debt, and so options and futures on debt on debt on debt, until Columbia, the gem of the ocean, arose, stainless steel and glass reflecting God's luminosity high above the world, like an altar on which was piled the world's offerings to the supreme value of certainty, though late in life he realized that he had closed the world down.

In spite of his promise, his certainty, his insistence, in spite even of God's signs that led him to the very source of creation, to that great, unimagined flow of the sweet water of grace announcing itself to him in its eternal alchemical battle with the salt waters of life, they did not entirely believe him, and, though using and conceiving of endless horizons pragmatically, the merchants continued at the same time to operate as in a closed world, calling his creations growth or development, as if the surfaces of his topography could be folded in on themselves, as if space were only metaphoric, and continuing their vain and vicious attempts at accumulating value at the expense of others, the individual's right to the pursuit of happiness, they called it, their buy low, sell high principle, until ten cents worth of wheat was ground and packaged in red, blue, and white packages with catchy logos and images of housewives grown elderly in their happy kitchens for $2.89 on the supermarket shelves and, better yet, four cents worth of potatoes, sliced thin with wrinkles and fried, packaged in a five cent tin, would fetch three dollars forty-nine cents, which, he would have had to admit, was almost as good as turning time into gold in the form of debt securities, if you sold enough of them, though it was he who had opened the way for them.

4

His imagination was a fertile field of stories, many had been told him, many more he had read, a larger number he planted himself from seeds picked up here and there, their origins long forgotten, but most simply came to him, blown immense, untold distances on tiny white wings, wafted, buoyed on warm breezes or whirled, snapped, gusted, and whipped by terrible tempests, came to implant themselves in his subconscious, and when they sprouted into his mind, they seemed to him repetitions of a former life, or rather of former lives, for each story was like a constraint upon him, making him someone other than who he thought he was, a character rather than himself, and to escape the determinism of each story, he had to keep changing stories: still, some stories were repeated, so that in the misery of yet another endlessly merging night and day of fever, the white-tongued heat licking the walls of his small cabin like the oven Satan was preparing for his sinful soul, tossing in the sour, pissy smell of his bedclothes, he dreamt the story he had heard many times in his childhood from an old woman he no longer remembered, her cracked voice a sing-song incantation in the darkness of his sleep that hid her face, speaking he could not tell what language, the voice solitary like the cool certainty of fate. Once upon a time, there were two brothers from Genoa, John Miller's Thumb, also called Giovanni the Coastal Navigator or simply John Cape and Crystal Ball, and John was rich and greedy, but Crystal the younger lived in miserable poverty with his wife and two sons. Through many adventures their paths crossed, but led by God's voice Crystal Ball gained the immense wealth of kings, while John ended by drowning in the icy seas of the North, a chastisement, yes, a chastisement for his no, no, he refused, no, brother Crystal, I have no money to buy cakes for my nephews, but if you want flour, go stand under the rain spout naked as we were born and roll in the flour bin and keep what you get, and he does, but his skin shrivelled in the cold, and as he bent over in the window sill to protect himself from the wind, the dried flour cracked and flaked from his back, blowing off a squall of snow to John's ha, ha, ha, too bad, better go see Renart the foxy gentleman, who lives far, far away, on the other side of the world, and he does, going farther and farther, until night on a high, rocky plain a fig tree wrapped him warmly in its wide, thick foliage, like the first parents, he thought, as he drifted into the deep sleep of certainty, I will surely be led to the home of my Father if I only persevere. In the morning, when the sun had warmed the high mountain air, so that passing out of the shadow of the tree he could take off his shirt to feel the warmth on his skin, he thanked the fig tree, and what can he do in return, why, says the fig tree, if you find Renart, ask the fox why I have no fruit, and he went far, far away the second day, through woods ascending so thick and entangled with fallen and rotten limbs that at times he was ten or twenty feet above the ground, which he could not see until he came out above into a miniature forest of cedar trees no taller than his shoulder, hearing the barking of dogs that issued from a small brownish bird, and above the cedar woods, past a field of perpetual snow where his tracks stained red, until that night he faced an enormous eagle, as large as a roc, who agrees to shelter him for the night, cuddling him under her wing like a baby all snug in his down comforter in his deep sleep of certainty. In the morning, waking, he thanks the eagle, and what can he do in return, why, answering the eagle, when you find the fox, ask him why I cannot fly like the other birds, hoving and wheeling in God's element above the deepest of deep blue oceans, above the deepest of deep green jungles, until spying the yellow sheen of monkey fur, I crash down upon him from above, breaking his neck, she lifting herself tall on her muscular legs to show Crystal Ball how she would drop, legs straight, upon the monkey, and it is a blessing, he thought, that I am Adam's son and no son of a monkey, as he went off that day, far, far away. That day he progressed along a great mountain range that, running in a straight north and south line for two thousand miles, yet appeared curved around him all the length of his trek, and he traversed a huge, expansive bed of thistles covering a whole plain, taller than a rider and so dried that it was impenetrable except for the labyrinth of paths made by robbers, he feared, and he passed over a vast bed of perfectly round pebbles extending two hundred miles in one direction and seven hundred miles in the other, encountering there such numbers of butterflies in bands and flocks of countless myriads, reaching farther than he could see, even through the telescope, and it seemed a snowstorm of butterflies that day, until he came to a stream, and begging the stream permission and for the love of our Catholic Majesties to cross over, he was answered by the stream that that was fine if he would ask the fox why I have no fish, and so he crosses and continues far, far beyond, until finally, smelling the sweetness of the air, he was certain he had come to the beginning of the East where dwelt Renart the fox. The stream will fill with fish, with sturgeon and herring, also trout, porpoises, rays, old wives, mullets, plaice, Miller's Thumbs, cod, salmon, seals, with bagres and dorados and the fish natives call bacalao, with palometas who will devour the carcass of a man in less than a minute, surubis, perch, pike, and big mouths and small mouths, bonito, turbot, and with varieties of fish whose names are still unknown, but only when the stream has drowned a man. The eagle will fly with the turkeycocks, the partridges, parrots, pigeons, ring doves, turtles, blackbirds, crows, tercels, falcons, laynerds, herons, cranes, storks, wild geese, mallards, cormorants, hernshaws, white, red, black, and grey, with an infinite sort of all wild fowl as soon as Crystal Ball takes the stone off its tail. And with this golden spade you shall dig up the pots that are bound in the roots of the fig tree, freeing it so it can bear all the fruits of the world continually, the year round when it is with leaf and when it is without, the buds and the flowers and fruit all simultaneous on it. And so, he does, skirting widely the stream which stretched its fingers out to pull him in but could not reach him, he returned to the eagle, and using his spade as a bar, he removed the stone from the eagle's tail, and as the eagle, taking two hops, leapt into the sky, the stone suddenly sparked, turned the blue of the sky, treetops showing upside down, dazzling as the eagle's eye, became a diamond boulder, light in all colors streaming out of it. At the fig tree, he dug out the ten earthen pots filled with rocks from under its roots, and when the tree sagged down to the ground, heavy with fruit, the rocks in the pots turned to gold. Whee, home safe, not caring who saw him, dancing in the rain, he arrived at John's house with his procession, urging him, too, to try his fortune there far, far away, and he did, but the tree was already full of fruit, the eagle soaring overhead couldn't hear him, and the stream rose up and drowned him, the palometas swirling for a moment round his body. Lying in drowsy dream off the coast of Nicaragua only twenty leagues from the largest gold deposit the Spanish would mine, twenty five years after his death, he heard the cracked Genoese voice call to him, Crystal, Crystal Ball, seek your fortune in the West, and he woke with a start, turning suddenly to the door, because he recognized that it was not his name but some stranger's name that was called to him, though even startled awake he heard her call him Crystal, Crystal Ball, go west, which could only be the name death called him by.

5

Astronomy is the queen of knowledge, for it tells us of heavenly doings and is measured in the abstractions of our thought, for it follows the steps of our intellect step by step into the eternal and ethereal things, for its language is the pure language of intellect, but among the earthly knowledges, navigation reigns, for navigation relates every moment on this earth with the things of the upper world, and although the Babylonians were the greatest astronomers, having built twelve tall towers from which their wisemen studied the stars, still, being landlocked, they had to give way to people of movement, for these could measure their traversals of the earth by measuring the stars.

Holding his unbreakable Fay's Drug pocket comb straight up at arm's length, he sighted through the fine teeth at the windows of the little lantern cupola of the Giralda just visible above the buildings from his position on the bridge over the Guadalquivir, another loony Japanese tourist no doubt, and found, by moving his head back and forth and side to side, that he could keep the windows well within three or four teeth, so that given, counting, sixty-five teeth on the comb, and, swinging his comb, still at arm's length slowly up, he estimated, five combs from horizon line to straight overhead, it was possible for Colon to measure the angle of Stella Maris above the horizon to within, five times sixty-five divided by ninety, which is three and a half teeth for each degree, so, to within a third of a degree accuracy if he had a pocket comb, and that is within twenty miles in terms of location on the earth's surface, so that, he ought to have been able, when on a north-south tack to hit an island forty miles in diameter, though if Columbus didn't know a degree was sixty miles, he could look through his fine tooth comb endlessly without knowing where he was. So, leaving the crowd on the bridge waiting for the Cambridge-Milan-Seville regatta, he returned home to look for Rihan's compass and ruler and drew his circle for the earth and, imagining a ship sailing up the hump of the circle, drew radial lines for two locations and parallel lines of sightings for the pole star, and, of course, it was easy for Colon, sailing a meridian south, to subtract the second day's angle, at three and a half teeth per degree, from the first day's angle to get how many degrees the ship had sailed and, if he had practiced with a portulan book in his youth on his trips around the inland sea, dropping a piece of wood overboard and watching how fast it went the length of the ship, counting the seconds in his head or tapping them out on the railing, to match his rhythms and estimates, like a soldier's marching step, to the distances given in his portulan book, then he would have known how many leagues he had gone that day and so know how many leagues were in one degree rise of Stella Maris, but on his diagram the sighting lines were not parallel, there being a small epsilon factor depending on the distance from the earth to the pole star. He might calculate the epsilon factor by taking readings of the sun and using Pliny's description of Posidonius' results that the sun was five hundred million stades from the earth, which is ninety-two million kilometers, and that the earth's diameter was seventy-six thousand four hundred stades, which is six thousand five hundred fifty kilometers instead of the present day calculation of eleven thousand seven hundred kilometers, which meant the sun's distance from us was six thousand five hundred times the size of the earth, very far away indeed, and since Stella Maris was on the orb of the fixed stars, next to the prime, musical, moving spherical force of God, much farther away than the sun, and since Colon owned a copy of Pliny, his epsilon factor would have been nil. On the other hand, Ptolemy gave the sun's distance at only six hundred five times the earth's diameter, which, though Colon had not read Ptolemy directly, he guessed, he might have

picked up in Pius the Second's works or in Pierre d'Ailly's, but even
with this figure epsilon would have been small. Colon might have
gone directly to Pius where that author supports Ptolemy's calculation of 500 stades to one degree, but, no, elegant as this whole
calculation was, Colon did not figure his distances with his comb.
Instead, he based his figures on something he had heard once on his
travels, that the Arabs said there were fifty-seven miles to one part of
a great circle, which he knew to be fifty-seven thousand paces, he
remembered reading, but how long was a soldier's pace, watching
the clattering soldiers marching down the dusty roads around Cordoba
in their straggled, broken step formation and again and again in the
principal plaza, which must be almost the size of a stade, their quick
march and half march, the ordinary step and the gala step, why was
there so much variety in the world, watching, counting, 120 steps to
the minute, was a pace one step or was it one leg brought forwards,
counted right-left-right-left or right-right-right-right, measuring the
prints in the dust, pacing his small room at night from wall to wall,
laying out coins on the floor to measure the different steps, but still
confused, because a roman passus was measured from the heel of the
foot to the toe of the same foot striding forward, so that a passus was
a foot longer than a double stride and a mille could be much more
than a thousand double strides if it were a thousand passi. But the
conversions were too many to keep straight, even using a standard
metric système internationale adopted by the CGPM, for he had to
consider the whole international history of weights and measures, or
rather the histories, for each cultural center perpetrated its own
measurements of the world, and within each culture the seamen and
the military formed their own cabals, so he had, like a Renaissance
banker with his coins, to sort through not just yards and feet, land
miles and sea miles, leagues and cables, but old Roman feet and new
Roman feet, English and French and Castillian feet, in which the
standard references were useless, the OED hopelessly provincial,
referring only to yards, feet, and inches, as if Brittania ruled the
waves, dismissing the league simply as a measurement used by
foreigners, though it recognized that the word lecua appears in

Anglo-Latin legal documents but apparently without meaning, old miles, English miles, nautical miles before and after standardization with degree arcs at the equator, Roman miles, Arabic miles, geometric pace, Castillian pace, Roman pace, stades, the measurement used by Erastothenes, Hipparchus, Posidonius, the Sailor of Tyre, Ptolemy, but whether Greek, Roman, Egyptian, or Philetairian stades, he didn't know, and when he had followed the conversions around in a great circle through all the units, using the figures offered by the Spanish Academy, he found the ends of the circle not meeting, for the Academy had mistaken the geometric foot and the Roman foot, so he ended with Columbus pacing his room, measuring his steps, until diddling the numbers here and there, estimating high here and low there to compensate, he came up with fifteen leagues to the degree along a meridian, so Colon must have used the same lecua he did.

When he had finished, he laid aside the planed, dark slabs of chestnut wood and stirred the fuming pot of ox-tail glue that had boiled all night, steaming his room so that water beaded and ran down the dirty, colorless walls, filling the little cubicle space with the familiar smell of thick stew, and when the glue came tacky, the large bubbles rose slowly to pop suddenly, peeling back upon themselves, he and Barthome painted the wooden slabs with it, stacked them together to dry, later to carve the heavy block into a sphere, to cover it with the mysterious opaque gesso, that dried so white you had to imagine its purity penetrating completely through the globe: Barthome then painted, following Ptolemy's descriptions of the Tyrean sailor's map, the black indented, wavering, jagged outline of the firm land, two hundred twenty-eight parts of the circle around the northern half, and with a string stretched taut around the equator and another around the globe at the level of the Canaries, he found the second only about two thirds of the equatorial distance, so that, on that parallel, a degree was only ten leagues and Cipango was only nine hundred leagues to the west, if Pinzon's story about the Queen of Sheba was correct, looking at Bartholomew's globe, look Barthome, the inland sea is a little over sixty parts, half the distance to the East, to Si-ngnu from the Fortunate Isles, the same as a sail to the Levant and back, which he pointed out to Fray Hernando at the hearing, look, your excellency, it is certain, though Talavera still held back with his Saint Augustine doubts it.

Martin Pinzon, he knew, had not doubted it. Saloman had two flotillas, he told Cristobal swearing him to secrecy, for even his brothers did not know the story, no one knew or ever would know, one flotilla from Ecyon Geber which was Hiram's fleet and another from Tarsis, one to the east and one to the west, and Hiram returned from Ophir with 420 talents of gold, while the fleet from Tarsis brought gold and silver and ivory and monkeys, though wisely Saloman had no faith in silver, so that 666 talents of gold came to Salomon every year, so much that all the furniture in the gallery in the midst of the cedars of Lebanon was made of refined gold, the walls of the gallery being hung with large and small, three hundred of each, shields made of layering beaten gold, where he received the Queen from Saba or Seba or Sheba, which came to mean the far south of the world, and when the Queen had deposited her camel caravan loads of gold, gems, incense, and the massive and fragrant trunks of the almuggin tree, which Saloman had never before seen and out of which he built two hundred supporting columns for his temple and for his gallery in the cedar forest, she asked him a set of conundrums she had prepared during her long desert voyage, to test the King's wisdom, asking first, where are we, to which the King smiling answered, bringing his two outstretched arms together in a sharp slap of the palms, we are in the middle, slap, halfway between East and West, the beginning of east and west, between Orphir to which the ships of Hiram go and Sypanso to which my ships embark from Tarsis, to which the Queen replied, and what is wealth, a question that pleased the King whose memory was suddenly awakened into the warmth of an ancient dream no longer visualized but still clearly heard, the voice of God saying, and you shall also be wealthy, so answering out of the warm echoes of his dream that wealth was in four stages, the primitive first stage represented by himself, for whom wealth was an endless source in God, the second stage of wealth was Tobalito Ferrens, who's that, she thought, for whom wealth, while still emanating from God, was built out of his own selfhood, his fear, his ability, his ingenuity, his passion, his work, the third stage of wealth saw wealth generalized, as a social structure of competition and was represented by Dick Whittington, the final and most developed stage of wealth was Colon's wealth of debt, the four stages developing, but like all processes, developed to allow simultaneous anachronisms, which was capitalism.

So she remembered Solomon, he continued his story, in the spidery but heavy brilliance of his gallery, the air wafting, it seemed, ever more scented with cedar balm, forcing her to breath deeper and deeper until her stomach ached with desire, remembered, while sniffing the cold, salt, weedy, rotten-fish smell of the spray on the far shore of Spain, remembered Salomon saying that but ninety-five parts of the circle to the west lay Sypanso, eighty, only eighty interjected Columbus into Pinzon's story, and remembered too the stories she had heard crossing the inland sea, from Plinius, in a cold and barren study, smokey from the ineffective charcoal stove, that years before in Rome a Cornelius Nepos had told him of a group of Seres from the province of Macinum in Asia that had drifted onto the northern Germanic coast and, being taken by the King of Suevia, was given as a present to Quintus Metellus Celer, then Proconsul of Gaul, and in Rome, almost two hundred years later, the geographer Dominicus Marius Niger had confirmed Pliny's story to her. She remembered also a later story, during the tenth century at the court of the Emperor to be Othon III, before his flight to Ravenna, his large head always held a little down so that he looked at her with watery eyes full open, his small mouth a tight thin line, slightly high above a full cleft chin, in Byzantine robes held on his right shoulder by a large emerald clasp, the triangular crown of the German Emperors fanning out like wings above his ears, the French scholar Gerbert on one side of his throne, his regent grandmother Adelaide on the other, nodding his head in agreement and approval as Gerbert described in detail the clothes of the recently rescued sailors, three of them, from across the western sea, thin and unadorned blue silk jackets padded with the white hair of some unknown animal, the jackets tied together on the sides, and described their bodies, which were small-boned, thin, their skin yellowish and pale, their noses pushed into their faces, and spoke of their speaking a strange language which no one understood or could discover, their soprano voices dipping and twisting in little bursts of alien tonalities: remembered, too, the imposing figure, barrel-chested, full red-bearded Frederick II, who was less interested in the Indians found off the northern coast during the time of his grandfather Barbarossa, than in describing to her his recent experiment in building a giant cutting machine which could slice through a living man's body lengthwise instantly, so that in the moments before death he could study the so many different functions inside the living body, or his attempt to discover the true Adamic language, which some fool in the barbarian north had claimed was Flemish, by setting two babies incommunicado on the African coast, with caretakers whose tongues had been cut out so they could not teach the children man's babbling speech, hoping that in ten years time they would find the children grown and speaking to each other in Ciceronian Latin.

Behind her, he heard Pinzon say, from the sheltered cove on the other side of the sandy dunes of the spit of land, she could hear the wind-broken phrases of Arnaldo with her pilot Pedro de Velasco, preparing her galley with silken sails and ropes for the voyage and singing tales from the off-shore islands of the Chinese bodies found on the beach of Flores, of empty canoes made from a single tree trunk, of carved canes and large black beans, favos del mar, and drifts of seaweed not known off this coast, of a large cup of cane wood, large enough for four men to share, matching exactly Ptolemy's description of bambu, singing the romance of Count Arnaldo, who, as in a dream, saw a vessel all decked in silks of yellow, gold, mauve, with silken ropes of deep blue, skirt the shore, the captain singing an enchanting song to him from the galley in a language he almost understood but which he seemed to have forgotten: and after a long silence, Colon told Pinzon that sometimes he, too, felt he was listening to his own story, which he was.

6

From the most magnificent Sire Cristobal Colon of Terra Rubra, Grand Admiral of the Ocean Sea, Vice-Regent and Governor Perpetual of the Island of San Salvador and of all the islands and firm land of India, discovered and to be discovered, Captain General of the Seas for the King and Queen, our Sires, to Messire Pedro Margarit in the newly founded town of Santo Tomas. I send you this message by Alonso de Hojeda, a most daring and chivalrous knight, along with eighty armored men, ten horses, and their servants, for the better fortification of S. Tomas, and hope that your situation will grow better by it. You must, messire Pedro, try to keep the material I send you away from the Indians, for I have heard that they take from you whatever they wish. If the Indians steal, you must cut off the noses and ears of the ones responsible, and in that way all will be able to see which are the thieves and thus avoid them, for they will be unable to hide their punishment. Item. I cannot send you more provision, so you must buy the food from the Indians, but do not allow the men to go to the Indians on their own, for they will cause all kinds of harm, and the King and Queen do not want harm done to the Indians, for they wish to save the people and have said so themselves to me, as you already know. Send Arriaga to buy food from the Indians, and let all know that only he may deal with the Indians for food. Tell Arriaga he must speak to as many as possible and always graciously and with words of flattery: tell the chieftains that they are powerful over untold numbers of men, that their body paints are brighter than the others, for the Indians are exceedingly vain, to the tallest he must commend his strength, to the shortest he must praise his speed, those with large noses have wonderful sight, those with pockmarks are beautifully dressed in finest silks of the orient, Fray Talavera is indeed the most learned man in the nation, and I swear the Tesoro has no match in the Christian world for understanding, he is a muscular Christian, the King and Queen rule over a land so vast and powerful they have countless Kings and Emperors as vassals, yes, he must tell them that, and our men are infinite, like sand on the beach, to frighten them, and he must tell them we have heard of their greatness and wish only peace with them. You must try to see Cahonaboa yourself to say these things to him and treat him in this following way: give him a shirt as a present, but be sure to put it on him yourself and likewise with a helmet. Then put a belt on him, this you must do yourself and tie a good knot in it, so you can seize him tight and he will not slip from you hands, and also seize his brothers if they be near. If Cahonaboa won't treat with you, send Contreras to him in Camboa, is that the name of the land, it slips my mind, perhaps I confuse it with Cambai, send Contreras and have him say that you wish to talk to him because of his greatness, that you want to do homage to him, that you wish to visit him, better to make friends, but don't go with many men, for they may become scared and escape into the mountains. I leave it to your discretion. Item. You must inspire fear and respect in the men, yes, you must, for otherwise there will be no order. The Indians are cowardly people, which is why they will easily be made slaves, and they will not attack you if the men keep together and in good order. Punish them harshly, I myself am hanging two men tomorrow for disobedience. Remember, cowards are the worst people, for when given the chance they are merciless: keep the men in order and make them obey you. I give you the same authority which the King and Queen gave me as Regent and Governor and Captain General of India. Item. This land is now a Christian land. Plant the cross wherever you go. Carve the names of our Christian Majesties on all the trees. Item. Messire Pedro, if only you could see the future as I know it, the strands of your heart would slacken and unwind from the weight of the chains that I shall bear. I will be betrayed, yes, by my companions, by those I have never wronged but ever spoken kindly to. Alonso, who serves the Duke, I will send to Court to further him, but there he will be my calumniator, saying that I mistreat the Indians, I who have ever, as you know, punished the men for their insolence against the Indians, but Alonso, whom I love as my son, shall be believed because he is fearless above all others, once in my sight walking out on a plank jutting out atop the Giralda in Sevilla. And even you, messire Pedro, will flee from me on the first ship home, abandoning our mission. How I must bear His cross here in the city of Isabella on the Isle of Hispaniola, the 9th day of April of the year of the birth of our Saviour, Jesus Christo 1494.

.S.

.S . A . S.

X M Y

X͞p͞o Ferens

He signed his name this way, conceiving it one evening on board the Holy Cross, meaning by the anagram a map of the whole and only universe created by God and in which he placed his undertaking, the Holy of Holies, Sanctissima, above in Heaven, each .S. a separate Sanctissima, the Father, the Son, and the Santo Espiritu, but together a Sanctissima of the Trinity from which descends the Creation, in the Beginning, A, the Alpha of things, and Adam, the beginning of Man, from whom spring the earthly Christ, the X, and M, Mary, and Y, Yosephus, and below them, me, Christofer, Christo ferens, bearing Christ with my pants rolled up, Christophorus, a giant prodding the ocean floor with my carved quebracho staff, the Child on my shoulders, pulling the ships along by cables I heave with my other hand, carrying on, continuing Christ, Christ's support, and above him the whole created universe of God, all the way up the anagram to the brooding Santo Espiritu, the dove, me colomb, a branch in my beak, flying, flying over the seas to bring tidings of a new world, so I am also above, I above and I below, I a traveler, a mover along the way, and the way is up, up the mound that protrudes above the rest of the world, up the earthly teat to paradise and so my motto ever is, now reading his anagram by columns from bottom up, Jhesus, X.S., cum

Maria sit, M A.S., in via sanctissima, Y.S., read going up the way, and altogether it is one name, as God is one, and I am one, but my name is two, too, Xristo Ferens, which comes from three, the earthly family, which comes from the four of Heaven, and so my name is one, two, three, four, a divine quatenary standing for God, mind, soul, and matter, from which come all numbers and all things, and above me is only seven, the number divine, for seven are the days of creation, seven the stars of the navigator, seven the parts of the month, seven the parts of heaven, which are the arctic, the antarctic, the tropic of Summer, the tropic of Winter, the equinoctial, the zodiac, and the Via Lactosa, seven are the sacraments, seven the vices and seven the virtues, seven are the parts of man, his generative energy, his voice, his sight, his touch, his smell, his taste, and his hearing, seven the parts of his voice, as the seven parts of divine harmony and seven are his humorous excrements, tears, snot, spittle, piss, shit, sweat, and sperm, seven the days of a woman's fertility, seven the months of a child's generation, for I have seen babes born healthy and complete in the eighth month, seven by seven are the words of my Lord's Prayer, seven the years I have laboured in the new world, seven hundred the number of islands I have discovered for His glory. At other times he signed his name de Terra Rubra, for Adam was red clay of the earth, the vessel of God, as he was, and as the sudden storms of the new world tore at his sails and masts, driving him here and there, he was more and more convinced that he was the son of Adam that was destined to return to the earthly paradise.

Unable to rise, or unwilling to, he could not tell which, he lay afflicted, scourged down his left shoulder, the painful beating of his pulse along the artery of his neck diving under his skin to unknown and unreachable depths and suddenly surfacing under his left eye, all along the left slope of his high bridged nose, throbbing finally at the very top of his head, yet pressing and pushing with his fingers and thumb, he could not touch the pain. It moved, changed locations, reappeared in ten thousand islands across his muscles and skin, sometimes in the very center of his overly large, humid eyes. He was sentient of it and of nothing else, not the heat of this thin slice of

jungle that kept him from the mainland of China, not the interminable rocking of the Santiago that threw him pressing against the
sides of his bunk, not the sounds of his brother's voice arguing and
threatening outside his door, not a thought of anything else, except
this affliction pressing out of his body, which he tried with pushing
fingers to hold in but unsuccessfully, letting go finally to feel the pain
flush over him, over the charlatan, the ignoramus, a hallucinator,
slave trader, liar, insubordinate, inept, calumniating sinner, punishing him, punishing his body from deep within, punishing this
oversized head of his which was the source of all his pride and desire,
burgeoning out ideas and plans and explanations and stories from
he knew not where, and so he lay, his lagartijo eyes shut, communing
with his soul, but at times the affliction seemed to come from outside
him, and then he could only utter dry, hollow sobs, surprising
himself, from the Pinzons, who never listened to him, using him for
their own advantage, from Hojeda, whom he loved like a son, but
who stole his map and tried to beat him to Paria, from the brothers
Porras, a conniving rebellious pair he never liked, forced on him by
someone, he didn't remember whom, Bobadilla, haughty and vain
who put him and his brothers in chains on the open deck, Ulysses
lashed to the mast, who never returned the two horses and two mules
he confiscated as the Queen ordered, Pero Alonso, Juan of la Cosa,
Francisco Roldan, Pedro de Ledesma, boys all of them, like Alonso,
his prodigies who all turned against him, and from Fonseca, who
even before his discovery was against him and tried in every way to
block his voyages, now the backer of every scheme that encroached
on his mission in this new world. They, not he, were the liars,
slanderers, the infidels, they who told him this was not the Isla of
India, followers of Amerigo, and did not Amerigo sail with Hojeda
using his maps, so who were they that told him Hispaniola was not a
day's sail from Japan, that Paria was not God's secret world on earth,
they the ignorant fools who never could calculate the parallels, they
who jeered at him as at Christ at the pillar, mutineers all, this
whining, nasal voice of complaint for a moment covering the island
of pain in his forehead, and that son of a bitch, he said to me he

thought I was in San Francisco, so I says what's that to you, and he goes, come on, just like that, come on. If only he could have a little pleasure in life, the pain would go away, he thought, but thinking, pushing the side of his nose with his finger, he could not think of anything that would only, solely, give him pleasure: what was that list of leisure time activities in the questionary he received from the alumni association, reading, travel, church, music, golf, gardening, that was what Americans did for pleasure, no wonder he was not American, boating, jogging, biking, community service and volunteer activities, yes, yes, a profitable way to be leisurely, spectator sports, hunting, fishing, camping, photography, scouting, winter sports, summer sports, others: that was his problem, he couldn't imagine others, though the smooth glide of tepid water massaging his body would be nice if Colon hadn't given him his migraine.

7

Whichever compass line he followed, though he could not be sure he followed any line at all while the compass wavered this way and that, Sanchez the navigator said he had watched the needle turn completely around in two hours, within a day or two land would be sighted, the islands were so many: 7,448 said Polo, of which he had sighted more than 1,700, though he could not be sure he had not seen some twice or many times, so filled was this Indian sea of islands never mentioned by Ptolemy, each one so certain of itself with its coast line so defined, the beaches, the jutting points of land, the mountain landmarks, that he could trace them on his charts in jagged enclosures, each different, an infinite variety of shapes and sizes, but when he left an island, he left all certainty there, as if certainty were that small lump of substance sticking out of the turquoise sea and that sea were blindness and pure void within which were no distance, no direction, no place but empty extension, so that like a blind man, he tapped and felt his way, waving his arms back and forth in front of him, tripping from one island to the next, not knowing when he did arrive at an island and slowly felt the protrusions and crevices of its shoreline where to locate it on his charts, or if among the infinite variety of island shapes he had not already drawn the new one, if it was not already there upside down or merely twisted to one side. Space, he discovered, was entirely tactile, or it was nothing, and his eyes ached to reach out and caress the things he saw, the bare, brown bodies, so that, when on the third voyage sight began to fail him, he could not work on his charts in the dim cabin but had to take them into the sunlight to rid them of their soft, impenetrable fuzziness, so that when he realized that it was his eyes that failed in the cabin light because Sanchez could still distinguish the lines clearly, he said, his agoraphobia burst in his veins and descending into his cabin, he wrote that for thirty-three days I have not slept, so anxious was I of our destination, that I have become blinded from it, never suspecting that he was the first human to suffer jet-lag, having passed five time zones, staying awake later and later into the night and rising with the dawn, and wrapping a cloth around his head, he locked himself in with his darkness, feeling his fear flush over his body, running his fingers around the cabin walls, the polished edges of his bunk, the desktop where, fumbling with his roll, he ate the food brought by the boy. But even after a week blindfolded, even in the small confines of the cabin, the moment he stopped tracing a line along the hard surfaces of things with his finger, a line he could follow in the space of his mind, constructing its rectitudes and curvatures, the moment he picked up his hand, everything collapsed into emptiness and his fear returned, groping fingers outstretched, until one day, through the crisscrossed finger-tracings of his cabin, he distinguished murmurings on deck and occasional shouts, quick snatches of commands and rushes of running steps overhead on the poop deck and through that, at first very slight and then, as the shouting of the men grew louder, a roaring, growing also louder, which he could not recognize, like rushing mountain streams, a cataract in the middle of the sea, no storm for the ship was still regularly dipping, rocking back, dipping again.

The sea had turned sweet, sweeter even than the mountain waters sold by water sellers in Seville from their large earthen jugs, each with an opened pomegranate in it, to give the semblance of the heavenly nectar which our first parents tasted in their earthly garden, said the sellers, holding their crystal glasses out into the sunlight to send beams of rainbow colors spreading, and tasting the dancing water from the bucket passed him by Sanchez, he found it was like it, cool and rolling as it flooded his mouth, slightly hurting his teeth, making them feel brittle and vulnerable, then the oily feel against his tongue as the sweetness rose to his nostrils with the slight aroma of lotus, the first man since Adam to taste the waters of Eden, for this sweet water was not of the sea, neither he nor anyone had ever spoken of the sea turning sweet, but had to come from land, even if the land were five leagues off, and such a flow of water from land, at least a thousand times as great as the flow of the Guadalquivir in April, could issue from no island but some great and firm land that no one had ever mapped, of that he was certain, recalling vividly the world map he had constructed from Alliacus' and Toscanelli's accounts, the world sweeping up like a gigantic kidney across which was spread the terra firma for 26 spaces as Marius said, crisscrossed by rhumb lines that gathered here and there in dense clumps, the ragged edges of land shadowed in blue and green, so the land seemed raised like a platform against the sea, and giant worms of mountains threaded across the huge open expanses of Asia, while six spaces off to the east, at its beginning, Cipangu balanced the Fortunate Isles that lay to the west of the continent, and hanging down like heavy limbs, the three pointed masses of Africa, India, and Mangi, and nowhere was there this bay of pearls, so large that it had taken him a week to sail across it and whose sweet water extended at least 10 leagues into the sea, unless this were a wholly unknown land, known only in fables long forgotten and lost in the babble of man's confounded language, lost for man's transgressions, driven from his memory as he was driven from this land, the flaming sword planted at its western exit, just as to the east at the entrance that had greeted him in the blinding flash that dazzled his blindness when, tearing off the scarf wrapped around his eyes, he rushed up to the deck, as he heard the great roar of waters battling, the salt against the sweet, and in that flash that restored his eyesight, he had seen the majestic Trinity towering over the bay, a greeting and a sign of restoration and return, as was promised by the coming of Christ and as he had hoped when he dedicated this voyage to the Holy Trinity at its outset. There were other signs as well: for example, the wall of water that surrounded the land, as high as their main mast, which, when he saw, stunned him, and as well as the other men, he had thought they would capsize, but through which the ship sailed unharmed, miraculously, while he fell on his knees in thankful prayer to the three mountains, the tallest in the world, which held enormous quantities of gold, while here in the bay pearls abounded and were so plentiful they could be scooped up by hand from the bay's shallow parts, or the natives themselves who, unlike the dark and barbarous Indians of Hispaniola and Cuba, were handsome, tall, quite as white as we, without barbarous habits of coloring themselves, knew shame, for they wore woven garments of cotton, and spoke a language pleasing the ear, or his readings of the pole star that showed they were higher than any place they had before been, or the fragrance and sweetness of the air that was indeed heavenly, so that clearly, he had been led to the summit of the world, the world's great nipple at the tip of which could only be the earthly paradise.

That night he saw another dream, which he knew from reading Plutarch was always a presage. The long, wet shingle beach appeared to him not a meeting of land and sea but the edge of space itself, and his body rigid, he stuck out into the nothingness, as over a cliff edge, from his waist up, stretched into emptiness lying on his side, and in the stilled emptiness of nothingness, his ears caught the infinite and endless tales of two-headed snakes with blood as gehenna black as ink, of palmitos as tall as ships' masts which grew nuts and wine and oil on their tops, of oyster-bearing trees, of Upupiara born of fish impregnated with the sperm of drowned men, who dragged their victims by the hair into the deep sea and there ate their eyes and genitals, as he had seen on those bloated Chinese bodies found on the outer islands, of Neucara, the island of dog-faced men, of Nicolas Roldan, abandoned on a piece of burning rock in the middle of the sea for having knifed the mate, surviving eighteen months on warm and sticky turtle blood before being picked up by a legendary Nicolas of Lynn, of Tobalito Ferens, left by the Portuguese to live with the Indians, instead building a network of trade between the sea, the desert, and the high volcanoes, of deaths from fatigue, starvation, melancholy, faithlessness, of suicides and strange, grotesque illnesses, of bodies torn and mutilated by men and by hunting dogs, and it all was true: Pedraria Davila boasted of having had two million people killed, in Castillo del Oro 2,000,000 died in 28 years, on his own Hispaniola a million people disappeared so that after ten years there were no more Indians to work the gold slushes, which was a killing at the rate of 100,000 people a year or about 300 people a day, 30 an hour for a ten-hour day, in paradise.

8

He kept reaching for some illusion of Columbus' character, even though he knew Columbus was a magician, had once conjured up a ghost ship in the glowing mist just after sunset in Jamaica where he and his crew were stranded for months, their own ships rotted and eaten away by the worm, and another time had extinguished the moon to frighten the natives, and so could change his identity at will. He had seen him once as a giant, bearded man, whose intellect, nevertheless, was superior to his brawn, sometimes blond, sometimes dark as the death his arrows carried, sometimes heavy-footed, stolid, and at other times lithe, swift-running like a young buck, spinning, turning, gyring, always changing, a beggar, a king, an adventurer, spy, father, comedian, sacker of cities, lover, navigator, moralist, tramp, martyr, murderer, soothsayer, sailor, merchant, thief, bigamist, a nemo, he said, no-man is my name, to the one-eyed, earless and toeless barbarian in the southern sea, blood matted black hair hanging about his face, a nobody, nobadaddy, counseling in paradoxes, the way west is east, the setting sun is rising, death is rebirth, leave-taking is arriving, we give presents in order to deal death, the walls stand when we attack but they crumble when we leave, the wooden horse will be filled with life. From his icy stratageme fire dances forth, and a long voyage through the islands begins. Storm-blown he wandered off any possible course except westward, towards the setting sun, like time himself, everchanging, accumulating experience, wisdom, progressing, as if he embodied the whole civilization, its contents and its discontents, heading

homeward, towards an enormous nostalgia, drifting sometimes onto
one island and then another, landing sometimes on some strange,
rocky coast to seek water and food, noting the darkness of the rocks
here and the height of the trees there, the greenness of the underground here, the yellow illumination of the sand there, and on the
first island, he saw a fabulous garden of palm trees, eucalyptus, plain
trees and cacti, flowering shrubs, fountains all about spreading light
in all directions in tiny shafts that penetrated the somber shades of
the dark foliage of the magnolia and orange trees, and in this play of
luminous darkness and colors was a river beside which sat a mourning princess, her features and posture familiar, reminding him of
another beach and flaming city walls, but her body was strangely
naked and dark, with arabesque tattoos. On another island, he
followed a well-trod path winding deep inland, off the fragrant
bushes and trees all around him hanging head-large blossoms, pink,
white, pale blue, as if in an enchanted land, until he reached a
clearing at the center of which was a small hut, the walls and roof of
palmetto leaves, and all around prodding and snorting pigs of all
types, black and white striped, peppered or speckled, giant, rotund,
pink ones, marbled babies with translucent skins, thin, ridge-backed
and hairy hogs, brown and tan and all shades of yellow pigs, congre-
gated in groups, their eyes, dark, dropping tears, all fixed on him and
in the hut a recently abandoned meal and a human head in a basket
hanging on the wall: on another, mountainous, rocky island, the
natives showed him human bones of an enormous size, remnants of
a vanished race of giants, arms, thighs, hip bones, and a skull at least
four times as large as his but with only a single eye socket: on another
island, the tiny natives, usually docile or frightened, tricked his men
into bearing them on their backs, like so many Jesuses and Christophers, where they clung so tightly with their tiny bowed legs the
sailors thus trapped were ridden to death: off the coast of another,
his ships were stoned by huge boulders dropped on them by a
lowering, giant, black bird, which nested on top a cloud-covered
volcano in the center of the island: off another island, short, squat
birds with human heads sang of love and peace and an end to his

quest so sweetly that, had he not been lashed to the mast by Bobadilla, he would have leaped overboard: on another island, still dreaming of a homecoming in the west, beset always by disasters, a man of sorrows, even shipwrecked once on a clear, sunny, calm day, the wild boar he hunted turned on him, wheeling to the right to ward off his spear with his shield-like right shoulder and, as the lance slipped past his back, caught him inside the left leg, leaving a clean, almost bloodless hole in his flesh, the skin pulled back and raised all around like a giant boil: on another low-lying, marshy island, the natives brought a tuberous root from which they made a finely ground white flour that could be used to make bread of all kinds, but his men were afraid to eat it, thinking that it might have been the root of the narcotic lotus plant: on another, where the sky was always blue and no storms or clouds ever darkened the sun, the grass, green, thick and full, the natives grazed herds of humped-backed white cattle, which his men butchered in spite of his prohibition, bringing on an endless season of northern winds: on another island, still sought by his sons, Diego and Ferdinand, one through the law courts, the other through scholarship, still followed by his faithful dog, Blazer, still wearing, like Ulysses, his high-crowned, pointed cap, he watched the sea whirling around into an inverted mountain, drawing everything towards its center, first slowly and then slowly faster, whirling the debris of his wrecked ship into a furious still center, this island was called Tarsis: on another island, the natives were building an enormously tall tower, four-sided and rising to a point, like a geometrical, man-made mountain, up the four sides of which ran flights of stairs so steep that, as he descended, each step was walking off a precipice into the warm and humid sunshine, or was like a giant stepping onto the distant horizon, and on the walls of each of the four terraces that formed the pyramidal ascent, the workers carved monstrous faces of snaking lines that concentrated whole, lengthy stories into stone images, and in these grotesque figures he seemed to recognize the burning city, the bodies hurtling from towers, the walls broken wide open, darkness, himself wearing his father's mask, leading his sons wearing his mask, followed by his father, crouched and wearing his grandfather's mask, a Roman funeral procession, along a deserted back alleyway: on another island, he met and held still for a moment a spinning dervish, who spoke out of his trance of his homecoming in fines orientis: on another island called Opar, the beetle- browed men with stunted, bowed legs lived in the ruins of a once magnificent city, dropping comfortably onto all fours when frolicking with each other, speaking an ape-like language of grunts, worshipping the sun with human sacrifices, and telling stories of ancient gold mines so fabulous that shipments were sent every six months half around the world. On the island Aea, the King Aestes guarded an underground room made entirely of gold, where he kept his blind father prisoner: on another island, he found the pebble strand strewn with the quartered bodies of faithless men killed by their wives, who for long hours into the night were hunted down by his sailors and raped, scuffles in the dark: on another island, wearing only one sandal, still uncertain of his origins, he ate the soft flesh of mermaids sacrificed by the natives: on another island, he was given old, yellow teeth to sow, and the soil was so fertile that giant, stalky plants grew overnight bearing long, golden fruits, which he harvested with his sword, but so fast did the plants grow that for every stalk he cut down two would sprout from the loam, their long, waving headdress shading his head from the noonday sun: on another island formed of several shifting, colliding groups of rocks, he lost his rudder and the pilot Tifio: on another island, the natives forbade him water from their underground spring deep inside a rocky cavern more than five miles deep, the blind descent and ascent along a system of ladders with one bucket of water taking a whole day, and though they killed the king to gain access to the water, the labor was so great no one would return through the long darkness for a second bucket: on another island, he lost one sailor who was stolen by nymphs: on a small island, completely deserted, he found a sheepskin hanging in the branches of an olive tree: on a group of enchanted islands he named after himself and the separate islands after places and people and things he had known in another world, so that the whole archipelagus was a microcosm of his past, a remembrance of Pinzon, Marchena,

Fernandina, the Pinta, the Santa Maria, Rabida, Isabela, Espaniola, San Salvador, Santa Cruz, Santa Fe, San Cristobal, the only inhabitants were the giant tortoises the sailors turned over to slaughter, four species of snakes, hissing dragons, goats, and rats, warring amongst themselves, the black rats against the white rats, the running dragons against the dragons of the sea, the red snakes against the brown snakes against the black snakes against the white snakes, and the ones that could swim carried their wars onto neighboring islands, so that soon some islands were entirely dominated by some animals while other animals controlled other islands, hoarding the scarce water and sparse vegetation, all the while that the sailors killed the turtles at will, hunted the goats, stamped on the snakes, smoked the rats out of their hiding places with blazing tar, and rushed at the smaller dragons with lances: on another island, while rowing up a silent river in the early morning light, the haze just beginning to lift, the sun making diamond drops off the oars, he saw a white sow and all her litter: on another island, he found washed on shore the decaying bodies of two men with flat, wide faces like Tartars, their shirts pale blue, tied shut along the side with strange fasteners that formed twists and curls, like tendrils of grape vines, a long staff in the hand of one man, of a dark unbreakably hard wood, so hard it would not burn, and carved at one end with a grotesque mask, a monster devouring a human head, as Alliacus said, or a man wearing a horrible mask on his head like a helmet: on another island, behind a line of trees growing so tightly together that their bark had joined, forming a solid, living wall out of which protruded entangled branches, twigs and leaves, he entered a cave leading into a complicated system of interconnected and crisscrossing passages burrowed into the soft earth, the work of some giant weasel, the rubbed walls still retaining a smoothness below the white crystals the water had begun to form, the separate rooms, smelling moldy, one like the other except for some broken clay pots in one and unidentifiable, black piles of what at one time might have been food or excrement in another, and a small mound of arrowheads in a third, but at the farthest end of one branch of passageways, he came upon a room completely filled with soft, silken wool, the whiteness, undisturbed by time or dampness, so completely and thoroughly white that he could not imagine its center: on another island, so many trees grew that the leaves and flowers covered the entire sky, forming an island of woods in the fugitively fragrant air, in which lived tribes of catlike monkeys, the trees, so many and so various, so vigorous, so exuberant, that it was a marvel to see and impossible to describe, the branches so woven, so entwined, with so many spines and thorns and sharp twigs joined that he could only make a short way into the forest by chopping a tunnel with axes and swords, though that short passage was enough to show him trees with beautiful, perfumed blossoms and odoriferous bark, others so wild that only the monkey could conceive of their use, others so armored with spikes that the naked hand could not touch them, others covered with ivy and creepers, others so completely dressed from head to foot with delicate filaments that they seemed covered with woolen threads without being so, others that grew entirely underground, only their topmost branches protruding above ground in clusters of hundreds of thorny, dark bushes, which when dug up presented an inverted root system where the main root grew thicker the farther he dug, joining other roots that became even larger, and all grew in all seasons of the year, the leaves never falling on this island so that the whole prodigy was to be seen and always unseen: on another island, the land rose so sharply from the sea all around into an enormous mountain that he could not land, and rowing slowly around the island, singing a hymn of praise, he saw that the base of the mountain was strewn with gigantic boulders that appeared to have been cast down from above during some great cataclysm and that the mountain had a path spiraling around it that was crowded with people, from whence he knew not nor how they arrived on the island, jostling and pushing to ascend the mountain, which reached so high above him no one could see the top, though it was rumored that at the summit was a garden known as the garden of Hercules, in which grew an apple tree with golden fruit next which was a fountain whose pearly water flowed out in four rivulets dropping down the terraced mountain on four sides to provide the pilgrims along the way: shipwrecked on another island, where flowed a fountain boiling hot by day and icy by night, he was attacked by short, black men with furlike hair and flat wide noses, and penises so long they hung in front or behind their bodies onto the ground like third legs, and laying about him furiously with his club, he killed them all.

A good navigator, as he thought he was, could stand on the poop deck and, like the Moré Indians of the Amazon smelling for the new year, squint his eyes and sniff the air to find which wind was blowing and thus to determine the direction the ship was moving, for all the winds used to have their individual flavor and the wind rose was like a map of his world, the Tramontana carrying the crisp scent of rocks and snow, the Greco, the musty taste of ancient culture, the Sirocco, hot and dry off the Sahara, the pure light of the Mediodia sun, from the perfumed gardens of the Moors, the Garbino or Africus, the lavender scented Mistral blowing from the parched plateaus of Provence, while the sun arched over this benign world from the Levant of gentle rains to the Poniente of squalls, but now his world had turned topsy-turvy and uncertain. On the crossing, the deep black sea was the back of a furious animal, full of motions that lifted and dropped the nao immense distances, crossing under and crashing against the ship but never seeming to go anywhere. Standing on the poop, he could watch the enormous waves approach on one side and go away on the other side of the nao, like an invisible body passing through the ship, yet the nao and the sea foam only rose and fell, the ship sometimes sinking into the sea as if dragged down by great weight, the water rising up and up her sides, until he could touch it from deck, and then suddenly the water would fall away, the sea sucking in its breath so fast he could feel it pull against his own stomach, and the ship rode, then, so high its rudder drew out of the water, while the wet, scentless wind blew first from one side and then from another, across them and into them, shifting without reason, blowing from all sides and surrounding him with nowhere, but when the sea changed color to this emerald green among his islands, the air was so full of so many fleeing and unknown fragrances, like those vanishing overtones of taste that are never recaptured after the first bite of cilantro or guayaba, the more one eats the more the solid vegetable matter filling the mouth without giving satisfaction, the fragrances only hinted at as a desire, that the winds seemed to map out on all sides infinite, exotic, lingering worlds, but these fragrances of paradise would suddenly disperse in the face of a fast-rising northerly, that swirled into storms, Saint Elmo's fires dancing jaggedly through the rigging, while the sailors tied flat down on their stomachs wailed ave marias, screaming in chorus with the angry storm, whose force and violence split the world asunder.

And still the islands continued, even though he knew that from the end of the inhabited world in the east to the end of the inhabited world in the west was but a small sea and that from India to Taprobana was a little way, so that ever since the second voyage, when the land they followed from west to east stretched for 335 leagues and still continuing, the officers swearing to a fine of 10,000 maravedis and their tongues sliced, the cabin boys and common sailors to 1,000 strokes of the whip and their tongues slit, if the land should not be terra firma, and still he had been deceived, he was terribly tempted to believe these naked people who lived on fish, who never went farther than four leagues from their houses nor traveled inland nor knew the world nor had laws nor knew anything, except to live and die, who told him there was nothing in the world except islands, but each time that he felt the weakness and laxity of this temptation, he felt also an old stubborn certainty that somewhere in this other world where lived these people who made the excrement of bats into combs with fine sharp teeth that melted like wax when heated but became rigid and sharp again upon cooling, somewhere among these dark, ignorant, pliable, parsimonious people lived the Sitos, the Batriani, the Gordiani, the Saces, the Massagetes, the Seres, in places whose names echoed always familiarly in his memory, informing part of his certainty and his nostalgia, Sepurga, Scassen, Baldach, Balasia, Cathay, Bascia, Cothin, Coram, Singuy, Egrigaya, Cambalu, Gyn, Achalesh, Mangij, Cygianfu, Guinsay, all names that shone in deep but cold colors, as if they were themselves precious stones, lapis lazuli, coral, camphor, margarite, polished and self-sufficient stones, so when he gave in, without admitting it to himself even, to the idea that the farther he sailed the more islands he would encounter or that seeing land and not being able to see around the landfall, he still should chart the sighting as an island, he was also filled with relief and relaxed with the sensation of having come home, because, in fact, after the second voyage, he felt more at home in the heavy humidity and sudden violent storms of the islands than he did in Seville, where from sunrise to sunset crowds of people, all of whom spoke to him as he passed as if he should know them, gathered on the wide steps that formed three sides of the cathedral, bartering, hawking, buying and selling shares, holdings, parts of holdings in goods, merchandise, ships, people, hiring, renting, lending, borrowing, dealing not so much in goods as in hopes and chances and anxious talk, promises, the cut of one's clothes, faith, interest, calculation, power behind future expeditions, planned, imagined, hinted at, guessed at, or rumored, this Sevilla which was his creation as much as the islands were his discovery but which his nostalgia for a home in the west caused him to deny, and in the end, the only home he knew was aboard his nao, in a closed cabin that smelled of an old man because the continuous northerlies forbade the opening of the ports, still seeking a firm land where the oar would be mistaken for a winnowing fan: ah, for those barren plains of Sericana, where Chineses drive with sails and wind thier canie waggons light.

9

Perhaps being on the waters for so long made all things of the land appear fabulous and dreamlike, so he stared curiously at the native, touched his greyish skin lightly, stroked it, as if he were encountering some antediluvian marvel.

10

He did not know, nor would he ever know, the terror and wonder which fell upon the Indians when they saw the paleness of his flesh, a fear at once reverential and incredulous, experienced also by the natives in Mexico and Peru, in the Molucas, in Catai, in Cypangu and Borneo, in the Philippines, as had happened in Guinea and was to be felt again in New Guinea, and perhaps had occurred in Hispania itself a thousand years before when the Moors met the brawny Celts, and in Australia and New Zealand, in Hawaii and the Easter Islands, for being so used to the skin of his own body as a conjunction of his own feelings of selfhood, the paleness of his midriff against the ruddiness of his hand, he could not conceive that for people whose skins were dark, whose skin had color, whose eyes were used for thousands of years to encountering the human form filled with color and darkness without mystery, his paleness seemed not whiteness or purity but passionless translucency, seemed an absence, as if the form were unfilled, empty, for if the skin were thin, membranous, and transparent, would not the flesh and blood that should lie beneath be seen, and yet they were not. His pallid noncolor seemed not to hide but only to contain the blown-up spirit of man, not the fleshly man himself, and thus the dark natives all over the world told the same story of the airy presence of these ghostlike forms and hid in bushes to see if indeed it could be true as reported that they shat and pissed as we do, smelled their fingers dipped in European droppings to ascertain, yes, it is shit, but still the wonder and fear lingered, for every white man was an inhuman contradiction, form without matter, pure form, a spirit from a separate reality, until years and centuries later, when the habitual presence of that paleness had distorted human expectations, and dark Mexicans and black Americans are unable to see their own darkness without a shock of non-recognition. He could not have known, because in his eyes the even darkness of their skin flushed and glowed appetizingly, seemed to give their bodily forms a pleasing rotundity, like a well-turned and roasted suckling pig at Christmas, with no metaphysical feelings attached, only the slightest desire to penetrate and possess the form, a desire countered by another slight wish to preserve the form in its appetizing innocence, so that he was genuinely hurt and agonized when he saw that brown, taut skin cut and flayed, the flesh swollen purple as if peeling back from the long wounds across her face, neck, and shoulders where Michele's whip had beaten the Amazon's flesh into submission, though even now lying in his cot a decade later, swayed to the rhythmic tugs of the ship's anchor line, he did not regret having given her to da Cuneo, and instead, remembering her huddled form on the floor of the hut, legs tucked, and seeing even at this great interval of time the details of Michele's description of how the Amazon submitted, he felt rise again in him the old carnal affections of vanity he had promised Padre Gaspar to resist, and he repeated his Memorare Novissima slowly, always to serve Christ, suffering tribulations, while he felt his muscles relax, but with the relaxation returned the general sense of debility he had felt continuously since Santo Domingo, when that braggart personally arrested him and ordered him chained on the return voyage, and though he had recovered his books taken then, he could not, except in moments of sinfulness, escape the nagging sense of death and old age which so suddenly fell on him, as if he had been suddenly washed in vinegar, as Samson must have felt waking, a weakness like the premonition of death, Hercules had died in the fifty-second year of his life, but more than a muscular weakness, it was spiritual, like a loneliness so private it could not be spoken, even here in the port of Santa Gloria, in his Jamaica, on this rotting ship, Diego and his brother Francisco plotting, always they plot, as Hojeda had, waiting for Mendez to send help, waiting for Thursday, when he would receive his second sign from God of the justice of his enterprise, when the spherical sphericality of the earth would be shown the world imprinted as in an open book upon the face of the moon, the first time God endowed him with this visible proof, this vision by what Aulis called oculis corporis, having been then almost ten years ago on that second voyage, on the Bella Saona, precisely the island he had given Michele, off the eastern cape of Espaniola. He could not have known, because the reality he belonged to was of only one level, its existence was only spatial, and thus it promulgated itself solely by extension, expansion, like Hercules's labors or Theseus's deeds or Jason's search or Aeneas's nostalgic fate, so that no matter how surprised he was by the luminosity bordering their long, hollowed, log canoes, by the finely woven papagayo capes radiating their green-purple-pink-orange in successive waves of shimmers around the wearers, by the gigantic, grey-skinned tree with large oval, leatherlike leaves, dark, dark green on one side and pale, paper-white on the other, the roots like hundreds of enormous serpents, twisting and writhing for hundreds of feet around the tree's base, by the dense, compacted, naked bodies of all shades and mixtures of violet, green, and amber, all the hues and tints photographed through color filters and catalogued for light reflectivity, now available through the Library of Congress Photoduplication Service at $1.25 a slide, the bodies sometimes painted half black and half white, split down the middle, sometimes in tints of red, chequered, or tattooed or scarred in spirals and parallel lines that followed and created the body's contours, no matter how surprised, he remained secure in his ability to account for this terra firma, an unchartered extension of the southern part of Mangi, peopled by Indians, no doubt distantly related to the Seres of Macini, whose king mustered armies of 10,000 elephants or perhaps related to the Scythes, who ate snakes, as these people do, sometimes were anthropophagi, quite true, wore gold ornaments on their foreheads or large silver chest medallions in the form of grotesque faces, like the ones he had melted by the hundreds in Santo Domingo, and this European, Western, reality protected him from the aberrations of the natives, whose realities knew no such expanding edges but whose realities lay on top of each other, flowing into one another, bound together yet separate, the way the stone-works of their pyramids were layered and yet held together or as the layers of skin and fat and flesh and organs differed yet were but parts of a whole man, and so these ghosts, these bloodless and fleshless and shitless beings were of another reality and not just from beyond the horizon, and so while their things, which were of the material of this world, their ships and their armour, their beads and their cloth, their axes and their manhunting dogs, their swords and their ropes and whips, their fire, while these things were susceptible to the magical power of this reality, they themselves, ephemeral and monstrous, were not, for the beings of a separate reality remained powerfully separate. But even as he did not and could not know the terror of the Indians, he and all the other Europeans could use it, attributing their success to the simplicity, stupidity, ignorance, foolishness, malleabil-ity, or insanity of the natives, as Diego Mendez did in relating to him in Veragua, when they were threatened by several thousand Indians, that he and Escobar had walked unarmed into the group of palmetto covered huts of the village cacique and browsed about unconcerned through the huts, in one of which Diego found hanging on a post a driftwood slab on which was mounted lopsided a skull, crooked and smashed, the lips and cheeks gone, so that the full set of teeth grimaced like a macabre boy's festival mask, the women and children leaving their abodes free to them, though not running away, gather-ing in groups, staring, standing in the clearings around the huts, the men, too, holding onto their stone-tipped spears but not threatening or organized, until he and Escobar had tried to enter the cacique's hut when the cacique's son barred and pushed them back and the people began mumbling and then shouting and forming themselves, but still unconcerned, Diego, that intrepid reader of Erasmus, walked to the center of the clearing, took a comb, a pair of scissors, and a hand mirror from his pocket and calmly proceeded to give Escobar a haircut, after which Escobar cut Diego's hair as the astonished Indians fled into the jungle, where they remained with their secret fear and reverence and pride, emerging five hundred years later only when they had forgotten their aboriginal terror of this other reality and instead fled from the too strong sun that might darken even more their already too dark skins.

11

Somewhere, unknown to him, lay all the remnants of the stories he had pursued his whole life, Sky King, Terry and the Pirates, the Shadow, the inner sanctum, creak, whooo-whoo, I love a mystery, Brenda Starr, staying home in bed in the luxurious dalliance of childhood convalescence to hear the second Mrs. Burton, just plain Bill, the thousands of comics he kept in his lending library in the garage, and later the Salgaris, Stevensons, and Vernes, the Rouletabilles, Fantômas, and Sherlock Holmes, the infinite but nameless stories he listened to or watched or read one after another in bed late at night with a flashlight, turning from side to side to rest the book first on one side and then on the other, only one hand needed to be out of the covers on cold nights, his shoulders sore and neck permanently bowed, humped, cormorant neck, from having lain on his stomach to read, head propped on arms or chin on pillow, and much later, the first time he lived in Paris, when he was supposed to be enrolled in the oriental language institute, at the Cinémathèque for three films a night, over four hundred old movies that year, his last fling with those ten cent matinees of his childhood, they were all there, phrases, titles, badly distorted passages, tattered bits of relationships, adventures, situations, images of smiles and grimaces, spies, heroes, villains, scenes, settings, moonlight saturating a rolling sea, a small group of picketing mineworkers across a desert landscape, clattering chains dragging their human ballasts of Chinese wetbacks over the sides of a darkened steamer into the brinish deep, still there somewhere in his now confused memory, and they were rising, like bubbles, into his consciousness, apparently released by some coincidence with the bits and pieces of stories hidden in Colon's craziness, and when enough coincidences were grouped together, they began to give him the impression of a narrative. The certainty and faith of narration informed the chaos of his research, and the coincidences, not just half hoped for and half looked for but half invented, multiplied, until he knew that his history was writing itself, as the events which whirled about the maps he had drawn in Mexico narrated the many Walter stories he had collected, or as the theory of the Mallorcan origin of Colon suggested itself out of the simple coincidence that the disappearance of Prince Viana of the royal Navarrese house in Mallorca in the middle of the fifteenth century could be linked with a Margarita Collon and with a San Salvador monastery overlooking a bay named Colon, or what was more to the point, just as history, and not just history but prophesy, was written for Colom out of the stories of his mind, by the conjunctions of the four meanings found in each word of the Holy Word with his four historical voyages, for four senses, quadruplex sensus, have the holy writings, so that when the Word says Jerusalem, its literal meaning is the earthly city to which pilgrimages are to be made, but whose allegorical meaning is the church militant, the meaning most important for enemies of communism, while the tropological meaning, the third meaning, always remains in the faithful soul, and its highest meaning is the anagogical one of the heavenly Jerusalem or the reign in heaven to which we all journey. And these four senses had coincided with his four voyages to the setting sun, for the first was the earthly voyage, which had a geographical meaning, having established the place of the East in the West and brought the islands of the East into history, while the second sense, the allegorical one was given by his second voyage, in which as the representative of the church militant he had been given the task of founding cities and churches and the overall conversion of the Indians, thus returning the church by this western path back to Jerusalem, and in my third voyage, I entered into the tropological sense, which is always moral, and arrived at the seat of the faithful soul, at the shores of that mountain where all faithlessness is purged, on top of which lies the earthly paradise from which, like milk, flow the great, sweet waters of the Pariah, past the Dragon's Mouth, and this I did in the year 1502, and finally, the fourth sense was shown by his final voyage, when stranded for fifteen months in ships too rotten to sail, besieged by Indians and attacked by his own men, he received God's sign that his earthly mission had been completed, that having borne Christ around the world, returning Christianity to its place of origin, completing the circle of time which Father Augustine and other theologians after him, and especially the cardinal Alliaco, say is seven thousand years, so that the earth being now six thousand eight hundred forty-five years old, time was near its end, when all things would revert to their heavenly form: thus his life had formed a quaternary conjunction in the West, a conjunction which could only be true if Vespucci and Caboto and all the others, Hojeda and Bastida and Juan de la Costa and Yañez and de Solis and Alonso Niño, a boy, all mere boys in their teens and twenties, were wrong about a new continent, an America, here in his ocean, a conjunction prophesied in the sacred book.

So it would turn out that Colon's story contained all other stories, his too, but only because he conceived of history as his own story enlarged and subsuming all the others, living his life as history, certain that because stories were stories by the constraint of event on event and person on person his life would determine all of history and at the same time be determined by history: the logic of history would be the necessity of his existence. And because of that logic he had risen from the ranks, from farm boy, canal boy, backwoods boy, store boy, street boy, luggage boy, with luck and pluck, helping himself, shifting for himself, brave and bold, strong and ready, struggling upward, slow and sure, could say, strive and succeed, until, no ragged Dick or tattered Tom, his sons were raised at court, playmates of emperors and queens, yet with all his do and dare, bound-to-rise success, he was unable to understand value or, perhaps, the measurement of value, because, on the one hand, he clung to the standard of gold, whose glitter lit up even the gunwales of the native canoes, so that in a luminous sea, these gilded outlines darted here and there like a school of translucent fish, while on the other hand, his style of rhetoric, promises, contracts, confidences, epistolary pursuits, had already woven the warp and woof of a wholly abstract notion of value, a monetary system of complex debts and doubts, so that wealth became, as suddenly on the banks of the Quadalquivir, a continuing, persevering application of rhetoric to keep alive the memory of some original moment of confidence, when something had been pledged against another pledge, and out of the copulation of words had come ships, goods, provisions, men with knowledge and skill, titles, deeds, land and gold, until a voice spoke to him out of a bank of dark clouds, or so it seemed to him, moments before the squall struck them so violently that the ship sank her leeward railing into the water and every seam creaked as if splitting apart, and what that voice said to him in that quickly passing moment was that Adam was God's supreme creation, the completion of His creation, the measure of creation, and after the Fall, the true embodiment of labor, so that man, a man, any man became the truest standard of prices, a slave is a note of hand that can be discounted or pawned, a bill of exchange that can transport himself to his destination and bodily pay a debt, a tax that can walk corporeally into the majesties' treasury, if only they will allow it, and eventually they would allow it, for that was the logic of the story.

12

The morning's dark calm reminded him of a scene he had forgotten on that first voyage, or perhaps it was a scene he had read in the Decades of Peter Martyr describing his voyage or an account by someone else about another voyager, he had forgotten, though now the calm recalled to him how coming upon deck at night he found the ship lying perfectly still, surrounded by a thick fog, and the sea as smooth as though oil had been poured upon it, yet now and then a long, low swell rolling under its surface, slightly lifted the vessel, but without breaking the glassy smoothness of the water, and sealed in that quietness, he imagined surrounding them, far and near, shoals of sluggish sea beasts and leviathans which the fog prevented him seeing, rising slowly to the surface, or perhaps lying out at length, heaving out those peculiar, lazy, deep, and long-drawn breathings which gave such an impression of supineness and strength. Some of the watch were asleep, even as the disciples, and others were perfectly still, so that there was nothing to break the illusion as he stood leaning over the bulwarks, listening to the slow breathings of the mighty creatures, now one breaking water just alongside, whose black body he almost thought he could see through the fog, and again another, which he could just hear in the distance, until the low and regular swell seemed like the heaving of the ocean's mighty bosom to the sound of its heavy and long-drawn respirations.

PART THREE
TRUTH OR CONSEQUENCES, N.M.

Llore por mi quien tiene caridad, verdad y justicia.
—Columbus

1

The ancient Chinese character for map was a rectangular boundary, taller than wide, drawn softly, showing the pliability of the
brush, but with strength and backbone, like the bamboo from which
the brush was made, containing, inside, the figure of a city in the
north, its old-fashioned ramparts a bit squarish, and to the south
another walled city, perhaps double-walled, the two connected by a
highway from which branched side roads, and though the usual
explanation suggested that the boundary was rectangular because
the ancient Chinese thought the universe four-square, like the
Emperor's domain in Beijing, or for that matter, as old Cathay was
designed, according to Marco Polo, he sometimes thought that the
character did not so much represent some abstraction of the whole
universe as it represented a specific map of two specific cities, in
which case the rectangular border was really the edge of the paper on
which the map was drawn, and perhaps, even, that the idea of a four-
sided world originated in these sheets of paper old mapmakers used,
sheets rectangular because the wooden frames for the screens which
papermakers dipped into the rotten, oozing colloidal suspension to
lift out the thin layer of pulp that would dry to paper were easier to
make rectangular than any other form, for his work with Columbus
had accustomed him to think that people's conceptions of reality
depended on representations of reality more than on reality itself,
directly, on stories, gossip, pictures, soap operas on television, yet
these representations were themselves dependent on fairly simple
forms that the nature of the representations forced on them.

Mapmaking must have been a fundamental form of representation, as important for the Chinese culture as writing, for this character eventually came to mean any kind of picture, including a portrait, and even meaning to plan, to scheme, to want something badly. In any case, he explained to the miners and cowboys who wanted intellectual stimulation at the bar, that was the reason he had come to New Mexico, because it looked like the Chinese character for map, a rectangle with Albuquerque in the north and Las Cruces in the south, connected by the Rio Grande, some crosses in between, and here we are in the middle, by the side of Interstate 25 in good old Truth or Consequences, New Mexico, so he could watch everything in the state go by, which was not untrue, for when he first arrived in T or C, had gone to the local library out of habit, and studying the statistical maps of the state, he realized that the old camino real he was on was still one of the major routes out of or into Mexico, over twenty-five hundred cars passing along the highway coming out of Juarez a day, though a position further south in Las Cruces might catch several thousand more cars that turn west on I-10 towards LA, so that in one place or the other he had a decent chance of seeing Christopher. He must have known that by some subconscious calculation, since he certainly knew that most people would not drive the long way down Baja or take the major drug route through Arizona and so Christopher, if he came out or went back to Mexico City, would be going through Juarez if coming or going from the West and through Laredo or Matamoros if coming or going to the East. It was a good choice. He could watch the cars going by and wait.

He had never told Carol why he wanted to come to New Mexico, though she probably knew that it was for some reason too absurd for him to tell even her, that his recognition of its absurdity made his decision not negotiable, that what he would not own up to her was probably a metaphor for what he would not own up to himself, so when he said in Seville that he was thinking of going to New Mexico instead of returning to his university to teach, she had not argued with him or even discussed it, but merely announced that she and Rihan were going back to New York. He left Seville soon after they.

There was no doubt that he would return to the US: where else could he go, Christopher tried to expatriate, but he was already, had always been, an expatriate. Halfway down the dark bar counter was an empty beer glass and a small pile of white egg shells, a memento mori, no doubt, or a sign of acedia, spiritual thirst and hollowness. At the other end of the bar, a man tipped his Coors into his mouth, hardly lifting his head. Jeet, he asked the man leaning on the counter, one boot perched on the bar. Naw, joo, the man answered, pushing his hat brim up a bit, swinging his whole body around to rest both elbows heavily on the counter, hanging. Outside the plate-glass front window, the dazzling heat, spectacular but not at all inviting, cracked and split the boards that covered the windows of the defunct T and M Refrigeration Service across the street, now a yarn shop, the sunlight so bright he could see no colors, though he thought the old T and M sign was a pale blue, so that the intensity of light gave everything a shimmering quality of imagined or remembered presence.

The sun would go down in another hour or so, and in another two hours, his trailer would be bearable, he calculated, so about three dollars of beer should get him through the day, three times seven make about twenty a week beer money, twenty-five for rent at the trailer court, ten for electricity, two for laundry, two for LP, luckily the winter would be only three months here because his LP bill would be over thirty a month in the winter, he was told, though then he would not have to buy beer to get out of the heat, about seven dollars a day for food make forty-nine, forty for the government and social security, left twenty-seven dollars for the irregulars, and he was getting better than minimum wage at the gas station, because he also did the books, so after a movie or some band-aids at three sixty-nine a box or shoe repairs, because he wore out heels and soles incredibly fast in the rocky, desert terrain, and not having a car he had to walk miles in the stretched-out town for groceries or to get his propane tank filled, two miles just to get to the station for work, he often had only five or ten dollars left at the end of the week, which he blew on a big Mac across the street from the station rather than saved, because, though he needed a car, it would have taken two or three years to get enough money together for a junk heap that he could not afford to keep running. Anyway, he could have gotten a bicycle but did not, because he knew that need and desire fed each other, Cristobal's story, it was the social history of America, so that he had to do with less than he needed, though it was strange that his desire not to live like an American, with the conveniences of desire, had led him to come to T or C to live like an American, not, of course, like the American of its own myths but like a real American, living in scarcity in the midst of a land of plenty. He had come to this extreme West, to the land of the setting sun, the aim of all migrations, the final frontier, this land of enchantment, the big rock candy mountain, where fish jump into the frying pan, chickens fly into open mouths, redi-roasted, houses are shingled with pies, the end of Columbus' quest, the new Jerusalem, had come as everyone else in this town had come, to die, one thousand five hundred of them dead in the past ten years out of a population of only six thousand, and still the population increased yearly keeping the town's only industry, sickness and death, going, the hospital, the VA administration, the convalescent home, the ambulance service, two mortuaries, twelve churches, flower, gift, and card stores, second hand stores to handle the worldly possessions, a bank, lawyers, insurance offices, realtors for the estates, not a prosperous industry, for the clientele was not wealthy, soldiers, farmers, clerks from small towns, housewives, car mechanics, salesmen, secretaries, construction workers, tellers, oilrig workers, fitters, framers, roofers, pressmen, school teachers, miners, cowboys, body-men, waitresses, heavy equipment operators, spot-welders, utility men, garbage men, washroom attendants, body guards, truckers, hair stylists, stockmen, felters, government workers, nurses, policemen, seamstresses, engine repairmen, living on a median family income of ten thousand dollars, over a third of the families under seven thousand five hundred, twenty percent in the poverty level, only a hundred families with combined incomes over thirty-five thousand: he was lucky with his principle of self-deprivation and the five hundred dollars he had left in the bank when he arrived, enough to buy the twenty year old travel trailer. They did not mean to come to die: they came originally, before the Depression, to take hot baths in the mineral springs, the hackers and the lungers, the people with kidney ailments, rheumatism, urinary problems, undiagnosable fevers, ague, dyspepsia, all hoping to leave their illnesses in the increasingly more rotten, increasingly more stinking communal waters at the thermal site, which they did to the sorrow of the other bathers, and now they come to fish, to visit the ghost towns, to spend a night or a week of their restless retirement on wheels, to wait for the snows of the north to melt, to wait for their doppelganger to show up, to take the desert's heliotherapy, to catch the yearly Ralph Edwards show during festival days, to wait for their RVs to be fixed, but for whatever reason they come, they stay to die, a third of the population over sixty-five, making a median age of fifty, turning the sex-age pyramid, mapmaking terminology, completely upside-down above thirty-five years of age. They did not bring much with them, not chattel, nor money, nor knowledge, nor ambition, only their complaints and their life long experience resisting desire and making do. It was a failing community, the small stores, the cottage industries, the restaurants, the gas stations, the fix-it shops, the motels, fifteen of them, the RV parks, nineteen of them, were forever going broke, closed, for sale, for rent, out of business, gone, for exchange, make offer, the old thirties type motels with separate miniature cottages boarded up, the fifties type motels turned into rancid apartments, dripping faucets and gas leaking from the old waterheaters, and yet with the steady influx of immigrants new businesses always took their place in the short wait to bankruptcy, failing being life's norm in T or C, and that made him feel at home.

The squat houses, a third of them mobile units, though many of these were built over, added to, repaneled, reroofed, so they no longer seemed themselves, lay scattered a few blocks deep off both sides of the long main road in small unfinished subdivisions, remnants of public works projects that came to T or C in the past few decades since the war, two dams and a major highway, developed to accommodate temporarily and then left to be filled gradually by the ever present retirees, and as he walked past one cross street after another, he could still see in the twilight the streets run into the dun, rocky hills that surrounded the town, just end abruptly a few hundred yards away, the stones and gravel falling in small piles onto the pavement, the dark tracks of four-wheelers and dirt bikes splayed across the darkening hillsides, uneasy sutures of man and nature. Since the main road took several turns to follow, more or less, the bends of the river, the various sections of the strung-out town were quite separate, in some the houses lining up neatly facing the streets and only a few of the outlying streets unpaved, but in other subdivisions, the grid pattern of the graveled streets was simply laid over the houses already set up in open fields, the houses scattering here and there as if dropped by parachutes. There were slums in Mexico City where the squatters were called parachutists, but they did not resemble these subdivisions where the architecture exhibited a determination to exercise individual choices even though the range of selections seems to have been very narrow, confined to the cheaper materials carried by the lumber company, low-grade dimensional lumber, factory-textured sheathing material in grey, tan, or white and grooved to resemble planking, mint green or adobe tan rolled roofing paper, cement blocks, hollow eight by eight by sixteen for walls, solid two by eight by sixteen slabs and sixteen inch rounds for walks, cast imitation stone siding, and discounted paint, eggshell with barn red trim, tan with maroon trim, pink with walnut trim, and whereas the Mexican neighborhoods were communally structured, one house leaning on another, sharing walls and supports in beehive-like efficiency, these bought rather than scavenged dwellings in T or C stood alone emphasizing their limited choices and commercialized tastes, and whereas the poorer and more squalid dwellings of the parachutists were amazingly various and even ingenious, these two bedroom, kitchen, bath, dining alcove, living room, low ceiling bungales were amazingly similar, in spite of or because of their do-it-yourself additions and alterations.

When he turned into the long drive of the Idle Acres trailer court, it was already quite dark. At night the sky was nearer, and the Cristobal range to the east and the hills to the west drew closer and pressed against this town, like flattened, stage backdrops. Inside, he turned on the exhaust fan and the television: while Jose Duarte's New York publicity agent orchestrated the TV news establishment at propagandizing this no no nonsense product of Notre Dame as America's stand against communism, a true liberal and sole carrier of demo-cratic principles in El Salvador, only bulwark against both right and left wing terrorism, he cooked his one-pan dinner, his cooking having fallen off drastically since Carol and Rihan left him. He tried to run through the figures he was still keeping on Duarte, two hundred some documented civilian non-combatant deaths in the last eight months, his memory, like his eyesight, was failing, peasants, workers, students, pregnant peasant women, a young girl raped to death by sixty-five soldiers, two men thrown out of a helicopter in mid-air, and the usual crop burnings, destroyed villages, collective tortures, indiscriminate bombings and artillery attacks accounting for one thousand fifty-five total deaths, while the guerrillas, against whom Duarte is the American defense, only executed, killed by minings or killed in combat sixty people, proving once again our superiority in training people to destroy, kill, and inflict suffering. Duarte's democracy-loving government arrested two hundred seven people during this same period, put away ninety of these as political prisoners in Mariona prison, where were reported one thousand thirteen cases of tortures, physical and mental, including electrical shocks, plastic bag asphyxiations, and skin freezings, all reported by Socorro Juridico Cristiano and six international human rights groups. The figures no longer stirred him to indignation, fury, despair, wonder, activity, just the facts, ma'am, because living in America again, he was succumbing to America again, because America had a way of breathing indifference into all who enter here, effected some numbing instinct in our imaginations so that the rest of the world became unreal and only something to talk about, like the starving in Ethiopia, caused, partly, by habituation, getting used to giant hulks of cars on superwide, glass-smooth roadways so quickly that already regular cars looked cramped and dangerous, puny, or caused, mostly, by America's geographic size and situation, so large and isolated that the idea of neighbors is as foreign to it as actual neighbors, reversing the European condition which makes most Europeans multilingual and international in outlook or the condition of the rest of the Americas, generally, in large or small countries, where the US has, constantly, to be in one's view and one's consciousness, which makes Latins and Canadians just as international as Europeans, or caused, also, by Americans' fixation on self-congratulatory individualism, o superbia, withdrawing inwardly from the tips of their delicate feelers into the comfortable, smooth convolutions of their portable houses: no longer responded to the events in Nicaragua or El Salvador or Panama also because he felt he understood them thoroughly, thought he knew what was the cause of them and why and how, had expended himself, his feelings, his intellect, his knowledge, his life, in that understanding until he was symbol of what he understood, which he knew was the way of thought, quite different from the way of action, conserving, always conserving through understanding, so it was only certain that what he understood about American action in Central America would continue to be true continually, and that was another reason, perhaps, he had come to T or C. He converted the couch into the bed, got down the sheets from the overhead cabinet, showered in the cramped curves of his fiberglass molded combination shower-toilet, another for his collection if he still had his camera, brushed teeth, pissed, and went to bed.

2

He had left unfinished his Cullumbus manuscript, abandoning Colon on the forecastle of the brig Pilgrim, dressed in loose duck trousers, checked shirt, and tarpaulin cap, a not so typical nineteenth-century American jack tar sailing before the mast and listening into the mist-merging still waters for the deep-down, Bible-ancient truths his sleeping disciples would not hear, transformed into a figure of the homeless, the wandering Jew, the flying Dutchman, Captain Ahab, a man without a country, abandoned to consider the irony of the final transformation of this man whose very homelessness, whose very lack of identity and nationality had brought forth the most rigorously patriotic of manmade nations, because even though he did not conceive of the modern idea of the nation-state, he created it, because on January second in 1492, a cold, bright Andalusian winter day, on the outskirts of Granada, Ferdinand, our Catholic majesty, conceived the idea as he felt the lips of the moorish king kiss his hand in humility and watched in the distant Alhambra the rampant lion and the castle flying together for the first time over an entire nation, no longer double, Aragon and Castille, but together as one, like the two sides of a coin, and decided then and there, the kiss of obeisance still evaporating icily, to send for the tall, weak-chinned Genoesian or Corsican or Portuguese or Jew, whatever he was, this man without a country, this man before countries, in order to consolidate the new abstraction by a Virgilian deed, an Hispaniad of incorporation, for freed from the Moorish yoke, Spain was not only the first nation of the West but the type of the West, the most western of nations, ready to fulfill the Western destiny of world conquest, a destiny whose historical correlative would be America, a nation founded on Fernando's invention of instant nationhood and exceptionally zealous of its self-protective, self-defining mythologies and structures and forms, and then and there, too, in the glaring light of Granada, the Catholic majesties planned to mint the new testones with the gold Colon promised, calling them excelentes and demi-excelentes, with his portrait on one side and Isabella's on the other, abolishing all previous coinings, so that the idea of nation, this new entity he had invented or recreated out of the ashes of antiquity, would undeniably unite the two abstractions of money and the centralized state. He had abandoned Colon not just to consider this irony, which was only another in a whole life of ironies, but because watching Cristobal become a larger and larger, an ever more comprehensive symbol for European history, he pitied, more and more, his human insignificance, and in the many spare hours at the gas station, between sales, inventory, restocking the pop cooler, racking packages of cigarettes, checking the charge slips against the register tapes, he still worried about the abject pessimism Cullumbus seemed to lead him to.

He imagined, as Christopher had once suggested, all the people of European ancestry in Australia, New Zealand, North and South American, Central America, Africa, which must be quite a bit over three hundred fifty million people, living back in Europe, the population of Europe nearly doubling, making it much more overpopulated and consequently more undernourished than China or India, truly another world from the sparse, arid hillscape spread out behind MacDonald's across the street. So, it seemed that Europeans were the primary overpopulated group in the world, though hiding it behind territorial expansionism, had shifted part of the problem onto other peoples, and with the problem some of the blame too, and while he imagined the slowly increasing undernourishment of Europe in the late Middle Ages, yours is fourteen even, the rapidly expanding cities with their drear streets filled day and night, fourteen and one makes fifteen and five makes twenty, bonfires in every street, and the sudden consolidation of political and economic power to protect archaic feudal structures, codifying social differences, he wondered what organic principle operated or could operate in this culture to create indirectly and yet certainly in the mind and emotions of Columbus that concatenation of bizarre geographical, religious, navigational, and historical beliefs that allowed him to find the means to release the inner pressures of the cultural organism, restoring its healthy balance for the time being, so that, as he wondered, it seemed to him true that the discovery of Ptolemaic texts, the exegesis of Aristotle by Benignus, St. Bernard's sermons, Aliaco's commentaries, Toscanelli's letter to Fernando Martinez, the shared ideology of Renaissance natural and spiritual philosophy, and the sum total of Columbus' beliefs were nothing more than the culture's inducements to its human agents to resolve its internal ailment, overpopulation, and as such, they were themselves unreal and illusory, bait in some larger biological game, and if such also were morality and ideology, delusions humans used to justify to themselves their hopes and desires which, in reality, were deeply but culturally rather than individually motivated, and if he or Columbus or all of us were but pawns of culture, then what was he to think of the scientific or political concepts of today's culture, democratic ideology, self-determination, or objective proof, empirical truth, or the physical reality of the universe, the depth of purple in the shimmering sky's reflection on the hot pavement down the roadway, what could he think but that they were nothing more than the culture seizing upon him and others like him, deluding them to ensure its own perpetuation, like a low swell sliding under the Pilgrim, slightly lifting the vessel, passing through and under her to bring itself, in spite of her, into the extended fulfillment of its wave pattern.

He had to leave Columbus because, for all the stories he or Colon invented or stole, he and Cristobal as well suspected that there was no story, no history, Colon's fate having been determined thousands of years before him by the lightness of the question ancient Jewish intellectuals asked themselves about their past, in the beginning what was in the beginning, a question which, once formulated, could only be answered, there, then, at that beginning time was there the beginning place, and if the beginning was a place called Eden, then all of time was nothing more than the story of the extension west of Eden from then till now, from there to here, no story at all, if the end is already in the beginning. You go down the road towards town, take your first left, and then a right at the next intersection, that'll take you straight to the lake, and the state park is about a mile further on, you can't miss it. It did not matter that a zealous bigot from Tarsus, a tentmaking lawyer named Saul, fell from his horse on the way to Damascus and losing his senses wandered three years in the Arabian desert, because on coming out of the desert, he was told to go west, young man, just as it did not matter if Columbus could or could not make an egg stand on end, because he would still one day find himself at the gate of the Rabida monastery overlooking the rio Tinto estuary, asking for a bite of bread and water for Diego, and invited inside, engaging in conversation with the prior John who turned out to have been the queen's father confessor, the queen's ear, as it were, so that on arriving at the Holy Faith Camp outside Granada with the queen's invitation, he was told to go west, young man, nor did it matter that a Chinese professor of the history of geography saw an apocalyptic vision during the Mexico City earthquake, because he would still have gone west to this land of truth or consequences.

Others had gone east, Cain, Alexander, Jesus, Thomas the doubter accompanied by mother Mary, fat John from the plain where horn-beam grows, Bill of Rubruck, the brothers Polo, Vasco da Gama, but they were simply wrong, following a mere sidepath when the deter-mined path all along had been to the west, but their choices did not matter any more than those of Paul or Colon. He had considered this, and he, obviously, was still considering it, if the past determined the future and the past could not be changed, then the future could also not be altered. Of course, Paul had said as much, that he was not his own man but served history, and Columbus, too, insisted he was the instrument of Christ's mission, and mother Ann Lee's path to America was strewn with grace, but he was not yet willing to admit it,

America the summa historiae, Christ's history of resurrection and restoration, returning mankind to a second Eden, the teleological end of God's creation, the created world's apogee.

Outside, at the pumps a converted schoolbus, large splotches of pink, white, and turquoise clouds and Jesus painted in dark blue, a dirty stovepipe sticking up midship, started sucking in sixty-five gallons of leaded gas. A thin, sandy-haired woman listened to the steady stream of gas while three young girls took advantage of the bus's shade, lined up along side as if posing for a WPA photograph in their loose Salvation Army dresses. The father perched straddling the engine, his head down in the carburetor, adjusting it while he revved the engine over and over, his dingy green, colorless butt sticking out of the jowls of the engine cover and his shrunken blue T-shirt pulled up showing a very white strip of buttocks and back. They were heading for Oregon after six months with their church in Belize.

He was not ready yet to accept that the strain of pessimism in his thinking could lead only to hallelujah, even if he had somehow come to the same conclusions as the Seventh Day Adventists, the only difference being that while they thought of themselves as winners in God's war with Satan, he was obviously one of the losers.

3

Junk filled the whole building and overflowed onto the sidewalk, where, for some unknown reason, Toby had lined up several of the sixty apartment-size refrigerators and gas stoves he had bought at auction in Albuquerque the week before, the rest warehoused awaiting his liquidation of the junk store to form the basis of his new business, just in case someone wants to buy one of these babies, and he would not admit that moving the appliances in and out of the store every day was a bother, no trouble at all with the dolly: four plate-glass windows stuffed with rusted fireplace screens, the built-in kind, their brass-plated trim bent and scratched, an old bowling ball, a dented trombone, a pair of wooden skis, a pile of AM car radios, coils of used electrical wiring, five bumper jacks, two electric stove tops, a green built-in oven, light fixtures, fans, electrical heaters, a franklin woodstove, tin bread boxes, a chrome-legged dinette set with torn red plastic seat covers, five kitchen sinks, a commode, and inside, a long glass case behind which Toby was sitting, thick beard and railroad worker's cap, reading some free religious literature. The glass case was filled with small items, jackknives, empty pistol holsters, medallions, some cutglass pins, fake pearl necklace, old wallets, a notebook or two, pen and pencil sets, cruets and perfume bottles, eyeglasses, plastic rim sunglasses, a blue glass eyecup, four bundles of silverware, a half-empty placard of enamel pins, a dented thimble, and on top were piled comic books, religious literature, more placards of enamel pins, a set of laboratory scales. The walls and ceiling were hung with crutches, ski poles, mattress frames, a dozen kitchen chairs, coils of hose, plastic water pipe, picture frames empty or filled with motel art, electrical wire, and there was an aisle for glassware and china and an aisle for pots and pans, all the cheap, thin aluminum kind, electric fry pans, roasting ovens, double boilers, coffee pots and an aisle for electric motors, car generators, waterpumps, jacks, chains, boxes of nuts and bolts, wheels, bald tires, headlights, speedometers, old wrenches, tire irons, an aisle for plumbing fixtures and pipes and elbows and joints and old, dried cans of pipe cement and shelves of condensed books and yearbooks and an aisle for old hardware, nails, screws, fasteners, eyes, hooks, and all about filling the floorspace between the aisles were electrical heaters, wheelchairs, piles of phonographs, defunct television sets, floorlamps, eight-track tapes and decks, flash sets for cheap cameras in their imitation-leather paper cases, artifacts of the culture, the lives of hundreds of people, each item the object of concern, sentimentality, or hate, all cheap.

Toby wanted him to inventory everything so he could sell the store complete, got to get out of this town, been here eighteen years, and got nothing to show for it but this pile of crap, in exchange for which Toby would give him the old Ford pickup parked in back of the trailer court, two or three Saturdays, no more, but Toby had a strange sense of time, he would probably lose in the trade, but he had nothing to do on weekends except think about Columbus and here, scribbling and making marks, one, two, three, four, slash, like an Egyptian scribe, he could listen to Toby, who was Portuguese, tell him that he and Colombo were paisanos, they had the same name, my old man too, but here in the damned Southwest they had to use the Spanish versions, like Colombo did, that Christovão had gotten most his information from other Portuguese sailors, who long before fourteen ninety-two had been sailing and fishing the Grand Banks, bacalao's Portuguese, you know, and where do you think that stuff comes from, from the icy waters of the North, professor, and that the Seventh Day Adventists misread the Bible if they don't work on Saturday because it says in Colossians, verse two, let no one take you to task for not celebrating sabbath, anyway Sunday was the Lord's day, domingo, and that's the day good Christians go to church, Saturday is for Jews and that's what it says in Deuteronomy, five, fourteen and fifteen, that sabbath was to remember the deliverance from Egyptian bondage, but this was an Adventist town and that was why he was the only second-hand store open on Saturday, or tell him how two years ago come September nineteenth he received Jesus in his heart, and he would not have gotten through his bad times after his wife died of cancer had it not been for the comfort Jesus brought, drinking, the store hardly ever open, didn't take care of the old man, bad, gone, but now look at him, he was going to start a new life, had put his father in the convalescent home, gonna get rid of this junk, open a nice used appliance and repair shop in Albuquerque with Gloria, whom he had met at the church, like an earthquake, shaken him to the foundations, and he had started to read the Bible, history, tracts, not just from his church but from all the churches and sects so he could make up his mind about them, for Toby was a curious man, and the more he read the more he saw that the apostate church, he had been brought up Catholic, had lied and bred superstition and untruth all over the world, was, as they say, a foul whore.

Toby, sitting on his stool behind the glass case and shouting across the room at him, told him that six sixty-six was the number of the antichrist and that the Greek words for wealth and tradition were the only words in the New Testament that added up to six sixty-six and those surely were references to the corrupted church of idolatry, and besides, the Greek word for Latin added up to six sixty-six, so there was little doubt that the Pope was the antichrist, and if that were so we were very near the millennium, even though it was not certain which of the antichrists the Catholic Church was, because in this century a second beast had raised its head, namely, communism. That was what it was all about, the great struggle in keeping the faith, what the Waldenses, the Hussites, Martin Luther, the Pilgrims, and all the others were doing, even if they disagreed with each other, lots of bickering between the churches, but they mostly agree on one thing and that was the struggle for the millennium was right here and now, in America, because America was the culmination of the struggle for religious freedom from the beast and so was founded as the protector of the true faith, the new Jerusalem, where the thousand years would take place, like it says in Isaiah, nations that do not know you shall come running to you, that's why the wetbacks come up here, why we all came, my people and you chinks, this is the nation of nations and it shall have dominion over all nations, that's in Psalms twenty-two. So, there was an agenda, first the preparation of America to be the new Jerusalem, where the sovereignty of the world has passed to our Lord and his Christ and he shall reign for ever and ever, Revelations eleven, fifteen, and listen to the word of the Lord, you arrogant men who rule this people in Jerusalem, Isaiah twenty-eight, fourteen, meaning the idea of the Godless nation shall be defeated and state and church, the true church, be coextensive, which is why the prayer in school issue was so important, second, the evangelicizing of the world, now is the time for preaching, not just here on radio and TV but everywhere we had to support missions, the church had to be nothing but a mission, leave your country and your kinsfolk and come away to a land that I will show you, Acts seven, Jesus then left that place and withdrew to the region of Tyre and Sidon, Matthew fifteen, all day long my tongue shall tell of thy righteousness, Psalms seventy-one, the earth is the Lord's and all that is in it, the world and those who dwell therein, Psalms twenty-four, Columbus's favorite psalm, continuing, for it was he who founded it upon the seas and planted it firm upon the waters beneath, and Luke one, all generations will count me blessed, the very passage Columbus glossed in his Book of Prophesies as a directive to convert all the natives in his ocean seas, all Toby's citations being somewhat familiar, he began jotting them down in the margins of the spiral notebook in which he was taking inventory, Matthew eight, many, I tell you, will come from east and west to feast with Abraham, Isaac, and Jacob in the kingdom of Heaven, another prophesy, Colon tells us, of his task of conversion, go on Toby, I'm listening. Third, Americans have to take up the armed struggle, confrontation, face the antichrists, aim with your bowstrings at their faces, he'd forgotten where that was from, the stench shall rise from their corpses, and the mountains shall stream with their blood, Isaiah thirty-four, the commies, the Iranians, Kadafi, drug dealers, and Isaiah thirty-three, whole nations shall be heaps of white ash, or like thorns cut down and set on fire, until, Psalm seventy-two, all nations shall serve him. I will set Egyptian against Egyptian, and they shall fight one against another, neighbor against neighbor, city against city and kingdom against kingdom, which he liked because it prophesied what we were doing in Latin, six sixty-six, America, Egypt's spirit shall sink within her, and I will throw her counsels into confusion, that's Nicaragua, and flipping once more his worn Bible to another scrap paper marker blossoming from the book laid on the glass counter, the land shall become blazing pitch, which night and day shall never be quenched and its smoke shall go up for ever, this is from Isaiah thirty-four, from generation to generation it shall lie waste, and no man shall pass through it ever again, which is what happened to the Japs, and these too were cited by Columbo, it was uncanny. Some of the churches had other agendas, like abortion, but his church hadn't adopted that one and instead favored American support of Israel, because it was written that Israel would lead the struggle against the antichrist, which they did against the PLO.

He wondered if Toby knew about Bill Townsend, jodhpurs and high riding boots, machete strapped to his saddle, missionary ordinaire at the time of the first world war, though one of the first to penetrate into the highland jungles of Guatemala, establishing himself in the eroded drainage slopes off the volcanic massif at about the same time United Fruit took possession of the lower Rio Motagua during the dictatorship of Estrada Cabrera, el señor presidente, among the Cakchiquiles, that is, one of the first protestant evangelicos, since the Cakchiquiles had centuries before been converted, conquered by the tall, golden-haired knight the Indians called Tunadiu after they had helped him defeat the Tzutuhiles and then given over to Bartolome de las Casas, saviour of the indios to convert, going regularly into the land he called Truepeace from his seat in San Cristobal, named after the man with whom he had come to this new world first as a young man and whose brother was also named

Bartholomew: the tall, thin gringo going in and out of Guatemala and Chiapas learning the language and translating the Bible into a new script he was inventing for that purpose until, nineteen thirty-four, during America's second major incursion into Guatemalan economy and politics, during the dictatorship of General George Everywhere, he was arrested by the Mexicans for unauthorized teaching and sent to Mexico City to explain himself, and in that highly anti-Catholic atmosphere after the Cristero wars and with a good deal of support by protestants in the Mexican government, he became missionary extraordinaire by inventing the Summer Institute of Linguistics, the vanguard of Toby's worldwide struggle, originally centered in Sulphur Springs, Arkansas, then with study centers at universities in Oklahoma and later all over the US, Canada, Australia, West Germany, Mexico, and more, divided into three sections, the Wycliffe Bible Translators, where written languages, and grammars to go with them, are created by the hundreds, over six hundred seventy-five now, and into which the Bible is translated, along with religious tracts, health and nutritional pamphlets advertising American products, contributors, no doubt, moral and political advice to inculcate the values of hard work and blind obedience and acceptance of the natives' lot in life, all published and taken into the field by the second section, the trained-in-commando-tactics missionaries of the Summer Institute proper, who are in turn supported by the Jungle Aviation and Radio Services. By the early fifties, when he tried to join in a mass evangelical meeting in Sacramento, the Summer Institute was openly anti-Catholic, going after those Catholics, and already well-heeled with support from major private corporations: today, he told Toby while they were struggling with the refrigerators to get them inside to lock up, they get money from the State Department, the Department of Health, Education and Welfare, the Agency for International Development, and on, have almost four thousand operatives, are established in twenty-nine countries in Africa, Latin America, Asia, and the Pacific Islands, have been in the struggle for the millennium for the last thirty years in every hot spot in the third world, operating against insurgency movements in

Vietnam, Kampuchea, the Philippines, Guatemala, Colombia, Peru, spearheading development of new oil fields or uranium deposits in Colombia and Ecuador by encouraging the natives to move off desirable lands and by training them to play their part as laborers in the modern industrial world, creating new markets for baby formulas, the dehydrated and distorted babies, stomachs bloated, bones fragile and undersized, starving because they will not return to mother's milk when the family can no longer afford Similac or Formulac or Nido, for processed foods, for American style foodstuffs, for American clothing, for American soap, soup stock, jogging shoes, cold cuts and white bread and mayonnaise and lettuce to make sandwiches. With more experience, better contacts, more extensively infiltrated into the local society than the CIA, the JAARS openly works with local military intelligence, in Colombia giving radio and aerial support to government forces cleaning out Guahibo Indians who resisted government confiscation of their lands, in Lebanon giving behind the lines troop movement information to the Israelis in their preparation for invasion, that was a fellow named Chris Dove, in Guatemala setting up a whole network of information gathering for the army's sweeps of the northern mountains. They were responsible for thousands of deaths, but they teach that each person is responsible for his own end, and that's right, said Toby, because salvation is your own thing.

Toby was giving him a ride back to the trailer court, but first they had to stop by the convalescent home to see Toby's father, whom he visited every day: look, don't ask him anything, just smile and nod and shake hands, otherwise you'll get him going, he'll think you asked him to tell his story, and we'll be there till kingdom come.

Most the people staying at the convalescent home were old, perhaps too old, having been kept alive by the culture's drive for medical advances but having outlived the culture's will or desire to care for them within the structures of society and so banished to this northeast corner hill above the town, living in institutional beige rectilinearity, low ceilings, identical cubicles, two beds each, the curtains pulled, the curled up bodies in colorless pajamas or nightgowns, lying on their sides, waiting, waiting and murmuring or speaking out loud to lovers or children long dead, waiting and calling for Emma to help, I've shat in the bed again, I can't help it, Emma come quick, or quiet and silent, no moving but waiting. In the long linoleum hallways, always a careful, wet floor sign somewhere, the attendants moved agilely through the slow traffic of wheelchairs, people walking with canes and walkers, shuffling people, and people just standing, staring vacantly or worriedly, frowning, perhaps supporting themselves on the handrail. Standing by the nurse's desk, a small woman smiled and said to them there was nothing harder than to remember happy times when you are miserable, leaning gently on her fingers balanced on the corner of the desk, a man in a wheelchair suddenly grabbed Toby by the arm, asking him who he was and why he had come before his time, and just as they were entering Toby's father's room, a tall, stately man in a bathrobe walked past, head held high and looking past them down the corridor, saying, infin che 'l mar fu sopra noi richiuso.

Tobalito lay half-sitting in the partly cranked up bed, a thin man with thin white hair and a long wispy beard. The skin on his face was faintly yellow even in the fluorescent light and translucent like the thin pieces he peeled off his sunburnt shoulders as a child, dried onion skin, tiny lines of green and red blood vessels seeming to lie on the surface of the skin rather than under it. He began talking in a high, nasal voice when he was introduced and he asked him, to Toby's grief, if the heat bothered him, and his thoughts found themselves a vent in tedious interminable sentences, that would have driven anyone into despair, and the thread of his narrative was broken by impertinent episodes that led to nothing.

4

There was something about the heat and the stillness of the air, Tobalito said. We were at only 7 or 8 degrees from the equinoctial, said Pero Escobar the pilot, and we all believed him, for he was experienced and careful and had sailed with Da Gama to the East, the ship moving very slowly through the oily water, and we all could see the asses' tails drifting by as we hung over the sides. Overhead, the slim, black and white gliders had for days announced the nearness of land, so that it was no surprise when land was sighted that evening, though it was two days before we could draw near enough to see the yellow beach stretch thinly along the thick green woods and hear the distant cries of parrots above the roar of the billows and some ten to fifteen natives, completely naked, on the beach pointing and shouting at Nicolar Coelho in the longboat sent out to communicate with them, but Nicolar Coelho was fearful because the Indians carried bows and arrows, and he did not draw the longboat through the waves but stayed off shore shouting at the Indians who shouted back, until at last Nicolar Coelho threw them a red cap and the knit bonnet he was wearing, and an old Indian, taking from his head a small feather cap with a crown of grey and red parrot feathers, threw it into the sea. Nicolar Coelho was able to fish it out with an oar along with a long bough covered with little white beads that looked like seed pearls. Unlike the Spanish, for we had heard that Colombo took many Indians captive from the scribe Pero Vaz da Caminha who was in Lisboa when Colombo returned from his first voyage and had seen the Indians he brought back, unlike

179

Colombo, it was usual for the Portuguese to exile someone among the Indians to learn their language and to inform upon them, and that night of the first sighting, the crew was gathered on the open deck to choose the exile. Three times the lot fell to me. I fell to the deck senseless, and when I regained myself, I found my master and, crying, pleaded with him to intercede for me with the Admiral, but he said it was useless and assured me that the Admiral would return to find me either on this or on his next voyage, that in any case, other ships from Portugal would certainly coast this new land, for all land south of the Fortunate Isles had been claimed by the King and he would certainly continue to send ships to explore the new lands, and he said many other things to calm me, and though I was not convinced that I would ever see the yellow hills of Entre Douro e Minho again, I ceased my pleading. The next morning I was given some provisions and set upon the beach. There were now upwards of several hundred Indians on the beach and in the woods beyond, both men and women equally naked. Some of the men wore caps of feathers, many had holes in their lower lips through which they wore short bones as ornaments. The women had beautifully formed breasts. They seemed not at all ashamed of showing their breasts or their private parts and many wore the hair of their private parts combed and partly shaved as if adorning themselves in their innocence. As I waded to the beach through the warm water, I noticed a man speaking excitedly, waving his arm and pointing to our boat. He carried a bow and some arrows and seemed to be threatening, but when the longboat reached shore, he ran into the woods with the others. Nicolar Coelho pushed me forward and yelled at me to run with them, which I did, not knowing where they were going or why, until I saw the old man who had thrown his hat into the water the day before, and running through the thick growth under the palm trees, I tried staying close to him, stopping when he did and offering him the yellow beads I wore around my neck whenever he looked at me. We came to a shallow river on the far side of which the Indians had stopped, looking back to see if my companions were still following, but when they saw me wading across the river, they made waving gestures as if warning me away, in spite of which I followed the old man across. There was a loud argument then between three or four of them and my old man, during which I stood near the stream watched by twenty or thirty more of them, and as I waited for them to decide what to do, a young man ran by me, snatching the yellow beads from my neck. I yelled out, running to the group in which my old man was arguing and, complaining bitterly, pointed to the man fingering my beads a little ways apart. Two of them ran and shouted at the thief, who turned and fled into the woods, chased by several Indians, who soon returned carrying my beads, which they gave back to me. I was then instructed to follow the old man who led me across the river and back to the beach, where I found my companions had already returned to the ship and, the wind being favorable, were getting under way. I shouted, waving my arms, but no one turned towards the beach, and feeling suddenly a great emptiness in my stomach, I collapsed onto the sand. When I awoke, I was alone with only the whoosh, whoosh, whoosh of the white-tongued water and the echoing rumblings of breaking billows, and the sun was already high overhead, the sand was burning, and my skin parched and red and painful to touch. I made no effort to rise until driven by the sun's rays I knew I had to seek some shade, and rising, picking up my belongings that were tied in a wrap, I walked towards the dark woods, but when I looked down the strand, saw how my loneliness stretched before me, I felt again the emptiness in my stomach and collapsed under the nearest palmito. In the evening, I found myself back near the river, the Indians having all disappeared, and being hungry from lack of food as well as from terrible distress, I picked a green apple off a bush by the stream, but as soon as I bit into it, my mouth burned as if with fire, and the burning spread through my whole face almost at once. I fell into the water trying to assuage the pain which was so terrible I cried out, tears flowing freely down my face. When finally I was somewhat relieved and calm, I reflected that not untruely nor without cause did Job the faithful servant of God say that man, being borne of a woman, living a short time, is replenished with many miseries, which some know by reading of histories, many by the view of others' calamities, and I by experience in my selfe, and thus reflecting, I fell asleep, ending my first day of the twenty-seven years I was to spend by myself on this coast far from human warmth or fellowship.

During the first seven years of his abandonment in America, this first European settler rarely saw the natives, running in fear when he saw them or hiding crouched under the thick, large leaves of the umbrella plant. He chose for his abode a cave away from the coast and the river where the Indians came too frequently to fish or swim or dance into the night, as he once saw them, spying from the tall grasses, envious of their joyfulness, desiring too to jump and leap to the sing-song chanting but also full of disdain for their awkward and uncontrolled prancing. His cave was high above the thick heat of the woods, high enough to catch the sea breeze and deep enough into the hillside to give him damp coolness all day long. In front of the cave he built a palisade, which at the end of a month branched and flowered, hiding his cave completely from view. In the daytime, he gathered the fruits and berries which abounded in great variety and which he had learned to distinguish, preferring the large knobbed fruit that was green when almost ripe but suddenly within a few hours turned yellow and dropped, which then, breaking it into its small sections, each containing a dark, smooth seed the size of the English farthing he kept by his moss packed bed for luck, he sucked, sucking the sweet, white flesh away, spitting out the seeds with a pop as he dug at the globules of roots the size of his fist with his quebracho stick that was so hard it wouldn't even burn in the fire. His fear of the Indians kept him away from the coast and the fish there, though later he went at night to gather mussels and clams and oysters. He fished the streams, but more productive were the small masked dogs with bushy tails, whose meat roasted tasted like pig meat. Birds he caught with a silken net he wove from a grass he found growing in a swamp, the delicate white silk peeled from the blades he twisted into long strands with which he wove not only his nets for birding and fishing but also a thin, fine linen from which he made his shirts, though it was too fine for trousers. At night he made throwing darts and arrows, eyeing them carefully and patiently scraping at them to ensure that they carried true, until by warming them in the fire and rubbing them over and over they became deep brown, glowing shafts of light, perfectly true, on to the ends of which he fastened bits of jagged, glasslike stone for those that were to make bleeding wounds, sharpened bone or fish spine the same thickness as the shafts, carefully smoothed into the shafts to make a clean fit, for those that were to penetrate deeply, and bundles of dried moss soaked in a mixture of beeswax and grease for those that were to carry fire, and these he sorted and kept bundles of each kind, both stored inside the cave and all along the palisade next to piles of fist-size throwing rocks and long boughs with three or four sharpened horns like deers' antlers to use as pushing poles, though he was never attacked. At night, too, Tobalito worked on his cave, which he called the Governor, digging deeper into the soft hill with his quebracho stick, his knife that his companions had left with him having long been worn to nothing, as had the four other knives he made from his metal dish and drinking cup, digging tunnels like a giant weasel to separate storage nests, one for the dried fish and fowl, another for the roots that could be kept up to four or five months, one for the gourds full of vegetables and fruits preserved in sea water, gourds as large as a man's chest, another for the cocos, another for the pearls he collected from the mussels and oysters, some white, some black, depending on the goodness of the water they came from, another for fresh water he carried up to his cave from nightly trips to the river, enough for thirty days, another for the cross he carved and where he said every evening and morning his Pater noster, Ave Maria, and credo in Latin, so he thought, intoning Madre Maria benedicteme and thanking God for the bounty of goodness with which He repaid me Tobalito Ferens for my sufferings, Amen, and another chamber for the wood he kept dry there, another near the entrance for his weapons and the grease he was collecting, thinking perhaps soon to have enough to make a mixture of oil and green burning apple ground fine and kept in fish bladders to throw in the faces of his cold war enemies, another for the curatives he had found, the stone from the head of the large fish that comes on land at night to eat grass and which is good for the colicke, the large-leafed plant with bright red stems that grows large white bulbous flowers standing three feet high once a year and whose leaves cause great pains in the stomach but whose roots and stems are a good purgative when taken with honey to offset the mouth-watering sourness, the small white flower with a yellow center, much like a very fine margarita but very strong in smell, which when soaked in water and drunk is good for coughs and all manner of agues, a certain kind of very fine moss growing like green hair under rotten logs which put on wounds, even when festering, will heal them very quickly, for fevers a waxy leaf from a plant that bore red berries and whose leaf was chewed by Indians with chalk for strength but which he found slowed the heart marvelously, bringing the fever under control, another chamber, at the farthest end of one branch of passageways, in which he kept his silken nets and linens with a large store of the silkgrass on which he worked during the rains, piles of soft, silken wool, so completely and thoroughly white that he could not imagine their centers, another where he kept his tinder box, his glass-stone knife, his yellow beads, the fishbone needles and awls, a small bag of copper ceitils, and far in the back and to one side and away from the other burrows, through a narrow tunnel blocked off with a large stone he had a small room with a few provisions, an extra knife, some weapons, and a hidden exit from the Governor onto the backside of the mountain, almost a bowshot away from his palisade.

In his ninth year, according to the calendar he had marked off on a tree outside the palisade, he discovered, on an exploration four days up the river, a bed of orange, yellow, sticky earth with which he mixed dried moss and turtle eggs to make a doughy clay he used to fashion bowls and pots, packing them when dried inside a large gourd with dried grass, seaweed, and moss, setting the whole on the fire to burn overnight to ashes, and thus, now having cooking pots, he expanded his eating habits and had to expand his cooking, for which he built another palisade enclosing a space twenty paces across with a cooking shelter holding his fire and pots of all sizes and shapes, flat, wide, shallow ones, bulblike ones, melon shaped and calabaza shaped, long oval ones, small breasts and penises, great pregnant madonnas, some with three, four, five legs, others leaning cockeyed with one another, lolling on their rounded bottoms, yellow, red, green blue, black, white, shiny and dull, their bottoms all richly burnt by the fire, and another shelter, built of pimiento wood and covered with grass, to sleep in, in front the ground cleared and broken with his quebracho stick and planted with maiz and dark green bushes of peas and beans and a tall shrub whose seed he had brought back from the mountains and which put out a bright red berry with a large seed that when dried and roasted on the fire could be ground and steeped in water to make a black, sour drink that settled the stomach and was good against binding, he drank the brew every morning, and this garden he had laid out like a great dial, the rows radiating out from a tall mast on one side of the compound, for he had realized long ago in his endless, dark burrowing into the hillside that counting the hours was life itself and the abiding of time was godlike virtue.

In my twelfth solitary year, I went down to the coast to see what God would bring, and reaching the strand, he looked one way, but far, far in the distance, he could see some figures in the water, so turning to my right I walked along the strand, keeping to the wet sand to avoid burning my feet. The sound of the billows was a relief from the constant noise of the parrots in the jungle. I walked all day until towards evening when the shadows of the trees had already reached the water's edge, I saw a large fish struggling in the shallow water. Its sides were all red and yellow, but when the water flowed off its back, it gleamed and flashed gold. Thanking God for His gift, I placed it on my back with great effort, for it was almost larger than I. With its tail still flicking strongly back and forth in the water, I began walking toward shore, but the more I walked the higher the water came on me. My feet sank into the fine sand at each step: the water rubbing against my legs carved the sand away. Soon the water was up to my neck, but I thanked God and continued walking, bent over from the weight of the giant fish. I walked all night. Sometimes the water coming over my head, I walked below the water, but I never stopped walking since God had given me this present. When the shapes of the trees again appeared, first dimly and grey and later glowing deeply, the water receded, and he came out on shore and rested, his eyes closed, facing the rising sun, he saw the whole field of sight an even, pure gold, the color the large fish beside him, now drying, was slowly losing, and speaking out of this yellow field, the darkening fish said to him, Tobalito, the path of gold is the path of God, his glory shines in all things, flicking out of the candle flame or flashing from the sword's blade, sparkling through the sandy grains or off the oily stains of your table, they are but types of His presence, windows through the matter of this world into His domain, gather the things that shine, polish them, increase their splendor, and make a golden world. The fish now lay still beside me in the sand, the skin peeling back briskly on both sides of his cut, first showing the pale, pink flesh, a thin layer, and then a black, delicate gauze so fine the two bladders suddenly pushed through and the innards spilled onto the sand. The glossy, maroon heart, the size of my fist, I cut out and laid aside still beating, later to be encased in a carved coco shell which he adorned with gold and pearls, the steady throbs echoing hollowly inside telling the distances he traveled on his voyages, for it beat only when he walked, stopping when he stopped, beating again when he moved, tolling his steps to the west.

As the sunlight glistened off the brilliant membranous, almost gelatinous, surfaces of the inner organs spilled out on the dark sand, he saw their complex interrelations laid out before him, the organs like golden oranges hanging each from its separate twig, each clustered in dark leaves but all branching from a single smooth trunk that twisted and divided and again divided, so that every separate fruit, complete and whole in its own golden roundness, was pendant from a single and unique source, as everything created by God hung from His benevolence from His body, and plunging his hands into the soft, yielding mass in front of him, this gift of God, he sorted the organs rectilinearly into their component complexes, a system of digestion leading from the mouth down a long, pink, almost white tube to the stomach, which was nothing more than an enlargement of the tube, turning there white and crinkled, which led to a small anus, a circulating system of blood that led from the tubes of the already detached heart to the spinal column and from there by fine, blue and red hairlike conduits to the brain cavity, to the eye socket, to the gills, to the interstices of the muscles by way of the bone structure and back again to the cut off tubes of the heart, a nervous system, whose transparent lines he at first could not see, tracing, though invisibly, a network that covered the whole body from lips to fins, from the scales to the gelatinous muscles of all the organs, the ossean structure extending backwards out of the cavernous head into branching and sub-branching spines through thousands of curiously engineered joints that had single or multiple or omnidirectional possibilities, some made up of only the merest of contiguities, ending finally in the flat sheaths of the tail and fins. There were other, more delicate and more diffused systems, glandular complexes of transformational alchemy, cycles of combinatory processes and change, all of which he traced on the sand in diagrammatic rectangles, and all these systems flowed into one another in a way which he fathomed immediately then and later constructed into a machine with layered and spinning wheels on each of which was drawn in circular fashion one of the rectangular diagrams he had traced that day on the beach. This great gyrating machine he called the Great Art, besides being an image of the totality of creation, was useful for making all the transformations and combinations that were possible in nature, as he demonstrated years after he had abandoned the Governor and this coast, when he changed the black sap of the earth that the natives used to caulk their boats into clothes, tables, lamps, paper, rugs, paint, bottles, watches, pens, eyeglasses, radios, Christmas trees, buttons, plates, an infinite number of imaginable things, houses and the heat and cold and light in them, cars, boats, trains, planes, and the energy to run them, or when he used a refined form of that sap to purify the twigs and leaves he had hoarded in one of the burrows of the Governor, leaves he used to chew with a bit of lye, rolling the mash from one cheek to the other, but, purified into a crystalline white powder, only needed to be sniffed to produce energy and laughter and abate loneliness, or when he drove off the weaker spirits from the dark brown pitch the Indians rolled into balls for games, transforming it into a completely malleable substance which could be made into any shape in any size and that was proof to water and to air, so that any manner of design that required pressure and either a sealing or a cushioning effect could be manufactured, or when he took from the tobacco leaf its benign humor by impregnating it with molasses and thus allowed the released humor to enter freely into any man, and on the basis of these transformations and others effected by his Great Art, he built his empire, though by then he was to deny that God had given him this gift, attributing his success to his natural spirit of adventure, to his bee-in-the-bonnet madness and inquisitiveness, to this mysterious energy I felt inside, prompting me always to new ideas and stick-to-it doggedness, to my five hours sleep a night, quick on my feet, always was, and never thought of the consequences that substituted for affability among his associates and made him admired and imitated.

5

In splaying out suddenly in front of him, the dark form of the ocotillo bush forced him to turn, struggling through some low growing mesquite, and to try to distinguish in the dark night ever finer and subtler shades of darkness, black on black, and the cacti and the rocks so seen, quickly and close and then disappearing, a myopic world, stepped over or gone around scraped against his pantlegs assuring him of the accuracy of his vision. He stumbled less and less as he saw or believed he saw into the dark world of the steep hillside, and it delighted him to find that he saw only by wanting to see, for any time he lost his intent, the hillside of brush and rocks and yuccas and chollas became simply an undifferentiated darkness, and still, even with this self-assurance, he was unable to say how many or where were the gradations of dark and darker in the deep interior of the creosote bush in front of him, even when he was sure he saw the masses of distinct little leaves and scraggly branchings, and unable to be certain that the rock outcropping just above him would remain there as he approached it, because in the dark, objects suddenly changed identities and forms as they rushed at him, and he was equally unable to say whether objects disappeared from his view because of his movement or theirs, or if they simply disappeared, and he could not say how far away objects clearly seen were or even say where the ground was while looking at it and stepping one foot after another without tripping. Seeing in the dark was a second sight which gave objects a home in a flattened reality not extending emptily to the infinite horizon but, being coextensive with the mind, embraced them with interest and will, as if seeing had acquired the ability to touch. He stopped to rest and found on straightening up that the hill he was climbing was not very big under the immense sky, whose brightness shocked him, and turning west he saw this immense dark dome of glowing darkness, sparkling with stars, extend over the stretched-out form of T or C's street lights below and over the wrinkled hills beyond, but he turned and began climbing again, because he preferred the hill's darkness which allowed him to see intensely, at the edge of vision, where sight penetrated the boundary beyond reality rather than furthered its illusions.

As a child he had visited a Buddhist temple and been shown the image of infinity through a magic window, but his mother embarrassed him by pooh-poohing the monk, pointing out that the magic window was nothing more than a dressing mirror facing another mirror on the opposite side of the narrow corridor, ho, ho, caught out again, you child of the naive East. He believed her, though humiliated, and though the monk was not, so that every time he went to the barbershop, he repeated to himself her explanation. Still, she had missed it, that mysterious wonder and mind-boggling paradox that inhabited those repeatedly miniaturized mirages of reality. It was the wonder of the mirror that captured the imagination of the West, as well as of the East, and produced, much more than in the East, worlds of images, virtual worlds, worlds of illusion replicated through the camera obscura, the lens, photography, perspectival geometry, radio, movies, television, animation, computer graphics, holography, each invention an ultimate in simulation until the next hollow illusion is invented, that was art, which in this root sense of ars, know how, backwards, did not even exist in the East, until now, after Columbus, replicated and also perpetuated through the narrative forms, doppelgangers, clones, we-hold-the-mirror-up-to-nature forms, history written as stories, stories written as history, true life adventure, dramatized news reports, until no one in this culture could tell illusion from reality, not the courts that decided cases of child molestation, nor the lawmakers who formulated the subtle differences between them, which, he supposed, only proved that they were just mirror images of one another.

Walking in dark night, several times a week since November, when he was moved to the late shift at the gas station, staying out in the desert until sunrise when he drove his battered, blue pickup to MacDonald's for a breakfast sandwich, piss, and hot water wash-up, lifted his squatting mind once again into speculation and concentration. Black was a color seen, but darkness was invisible: so, walking, he dwelt in an invisible land, seeing the unseen, not unlike the early travelers who felt their ways into the non-existent and returned, drawing out their itineraries on tablecloths to the shape of the remembered movements of their bodies, a veering to the left side here in the stand of dogwoods and here a passage through a steep ravine, the mountain on the left turned upside-down, falling away, like the picture-maps he had studied so long ago in Mexico but much earlier, before geography, before astronomy, before earth measurement had created projection maps, before perspective drawing had been added to create painting, before illusion, in the still, dark world.

When his legs lost what little spring was left in them and his feet, become toe-less and club-like, struck the ground hard and flat, taking his full weight at each step, hitting the uneven, rocky ground carelessly, as if confident in the earth's firmness, so that his ankles did not respond to the slipping stones or the sharp angles of the ground but simply pivoted his body forward for the next step without bothering to adjust to the terrain, and his breath came pounding hard through his chapped lips and crossing a gully he had to jump forward against the facing incline so that the momentum would bring his other foot forward to take the next step, because he knew that he could not depend on his cramped thigh muscle to lift his body up enough to bring his other leg forward, each crossing being a small spurt and then a hovering hesitation to see if he would fall backwards or forwards, tottering and then continuing, breathing more and more painfully, head down, sometimes forced to take a few quick steps backwards to maintain his balance, because sometimes the circuits of his body crossed and he would lift his leg and straighten up to take a step and find himself unable to put his foot down, falling backwards down the hill, when he was so exhausted that the clump, clump, clump of his body was all his thought, nothing but the repeated, automatic, careless, flatfooted stamping of his feet, then he saw them running in the high, granite, wind-blown mountain above the distant stands of pines but below the lines of rocky cliffs and outcroppings, their elegant, lean legs moving rhythmically, almost slowly, running and running and running, silently in the wind, the red and white blouses blossoming in the light air, until coming upon the blood-smeared ball, one of them stops, the others paying no attention, not breaking stride, run on, down, up, across the gully, as he puts his bare right foot on the ball, rolls it quickly onto the top of his foot and heaves it high, arching to fall among his running fellows ahead, where another runner stops, the others paying no attention, not breaking stride, run on, down, up, across the hillside, along the granite outcropping, and the new kicker heaves the wooden ball in his turn and on so for the day and the next and the next, until one team beats the other back to the starting point, and still not saying anything, not cheering or leaping, the winners pick up the betting money, flapping in the breeze under some stones, and continue down the hill to their wooden shacks or walled-off cave dwellings next to their small parcels of corn and goatsheds, food and shelter, and then he saw them dance their solitary, ritual offerings of food to the earth and join their wives and children and tribesmen in their difficult life.

The sun rose behind the mountain he had just descended, restored it to its distant place on the other side of the river. Slumped over his styrofoam cup of coffee, he used to drink buttermilk out of an elegant blue ceramic cup, he watched Tom fill the cigarette racks across the street. He would be doing that in the evening. Perhaps, then, Christopher would pull into the station, in a refurbished telephone van, the stripes barely painted over, the valves clacking a little just before he switched the engine off, and after pumping his gas and paying, say that his friend Sr. Muñoz had spoken of him, yes, and he had a great many things to say to him, the first was that he was old enough to be your father and the second was that the Quiche prince Tecum-Tecum had turned himself into an eagle, growing feathers on his arms and thighs, feathers that grew by themselves and were not stuck on, said the Mayan scribe, and wearing a mirror-like emerald on his chest and another on his back to repel the brightness of the invaders, wings grown out of his body, three crowns on his head, dove from high above with flint lance held steady, with one stroke cutting off the head of golden hair Tunadiu's horse, and rising a second time, wheeling to a rest on high, turning with half-folded, arched wings, dropped again, this time, at his utmost speed, to be impaled on solar-hair Tunadiu's steel spear, which is an allegory, he explained, not about weapons and technology, nor about strength, but about two realities, one founded on the certainty of supposition, while supposition for the other was only the unpleasant past, the rag heap from which the universe sprang, the first term of a clear logic that led to the final term of certainty, and whereas magic was the certainty of one reality, death was the certainty of the other. There might be a path which begins in certainty and whose final goal is supposition, but he had not been able to elaborate it, had not found it, and so, speaking as a father, was passing on this task to him, because though he had walked without a path, he had somehow gotten to the extreme west and could go no farther without beginning again in the east.

He was not concerned that Christopher might not arrive that night, it would be at night in any case, and if Christopher had already passed by, then he would wait for his return, and if he did not come at all, he would still wait, for his meeting with Christopher was for Christopher's sake and affected his life not at all. For himself, he had only to wait to become American or to die in peace, and he had prepared for both by coming to T or C. He wondered if he should impose on Carol and Rihan by asking that on his headstone they grave,

Jacet Kris Ng
He walked abroad

RECENT TITLES FROM FC2

From the District File
A novel by Kenneth Bernard
From the District File depicts a bureaucratic world of supercontrolled oppressiveness in the not-too-distant future. *Publishers Weekly* calls Bernard's fiction "a confrontation with the inexpressible...a provocative comment on the restrictiveness and pretension of our lives."
128 pages, Cloth: $18.95, Paper: $8.95

Double or Nothing
A novel by Raymond Federman
"Invention of this quality ranks the book among the fictional masterpieces of our age...I have read *Double or Nothing* several times and am not finished with it yet, for it is filled with the kinds of allusion and complexity that scholars will feast upon for years. Were literature a stock market, I'd invest in this book—Richard Kostelanetz
320 pages, Paper: $10.95

F/32
A novel by Eurudice
F/32 is a wild, eccentric, Rabaelaisian romp through most forms of amorous excess. But, it is also a troubling tale orbiting around a public sexual assault on the streets of Manhattan. Between the poles of desire and butchery, the novel and Ela sail, the awed reader going along for one of the most dazzling rides in recent American fiction.
250 pages, Cloth: $18.95, Paper, $8.95

Trigger Dance
Stories by Diane Glancy
"Diane Glancy writes with poetic knowledge of Native Americans...The characters of *Trigger Dance* do an intricate dance that forms wonderful new story patterns. With musical language, Diane Glancy teaches us to hear ancient American refrains amidst familiar American sounds. A beautiful book."—Maxine Hong Kingston
250 pages, Cloth: $18.95, Paper: $8.95

Is It Sexual Harassment Yet?
Stories by Cris Mazza
"The stories...continually surprise, delight, disturb, and amuse. Mazza's 'realism' captures the eerie surrealism of violence and repressed sexuality in her characters' lives."—Larry McCaffery
150 pages, Cloth: $18.95, Paper: 8.95

Napoleon's Mare
A novella by Lou Robinson

Napoleon's Mare, thirteen chapters and a section of prose poems is a diatribe, a discontinuous narrative—as much about writing as about the bewildering process of constructing a self.

186 pages, Cloth: $18.95, Paper: $8.95

Valentino's Hair
A novel by Yvonne Sapia

"Intense and magical, *Valentino's Hair* vividly creates an America intoxicated by love and death. Sapia brilliantly renders the vitality and tensions in the Puerto Rican community in 1920s New York City."—Jerome Stern. Picked as one of the top 25 books for 1991 by Publishers Weekly.

162 pages, Cloth: $18.95, Paper: $8.95

Mermaids for Attila
Stories by Jacques Servin

Mermaids for Attila is a fun, hands-on, toy-like book on the subject of well-orchestrated national behaviors. In it Servin considers the biggest horrors and the weirdest political truths. "At a time when conventional narrative fiction is making an utterly boring comeback, it is a relief to find writers like Jacques Servin who are willing to acknowledge that verbal representation can no longer be regarded as anything more than a point of departure."—Stephen-Paul Martin

128 pages, Cloth: $18.95, Paper: $8.95

Hearsay
A novel by Peter Spielberg

Hearsay is a darkly comic account of the misadventures of one Lemuel Grosz from youthbed to deathbed. In its blending of reality and irreality, *Hearsay* present a life the way we winess the life of another: from a certain distance, catching a glimpse here, a revelation there.

275 pages, Cloth: $18.95, Paper: $8.95

Close Your Eyes and Think of Dublin: Portrait of a Girl
A novel by Kathryn Thompson

A brilliant Joycean hallucination of a book in which the richness of Leopold Bloom's inner life is found in a young American girl experiencing most of the things that vexed James Joyce: sex, church, and oppression.

197 pages, Cloth: $18.95, Paper: $8.95

Books may be ordered through the Talman Company, 150 Fifth Avenue, New York, NY 10011.

For a catalog listing all books published by Fiction Collective, write to Fiction Collective Two, Department of English, Illinois State University, Normal, IL 61761-6901.